HEARTLESS GOON 2

**Lock Down Publications and Ca$h
Presents**
HEARTLESS GOON 2
A Novel by *GHOST*

Lock Down Publications

P.O. Box 870494
Mesquite, Tx 75187

Visit our website @
www.lockdownpublications.com

Lock Down Publications
Like our page on Facebook: Lock Down Publications @
www.facebook.com/lockdownpublications.ldp
Cover design and layout by: **Dynasty Cover Me**
Book interior design by: **Shawn Walker**
Edited by: **Lashonda Johnson**

Stay Connected with Us!

Text **LOCKDOWN** to 22828 to stay up-to-date with new releases, sneak peaks, contests and more…

Thank you.

Submission Guideline.

Submit the first three chapters of your completed manuscript to ldpsubmissions@gmail.com, subject line: Your book's title. The manuscript must be in a .doc file and sent as an attachment. Document should be in Times New Roman, double spaced and in size 12 font. Also, provide your synopsis and full contact information. If sending multiple submissions, they must each be in a separate email.

Have a story but no way to send it electronically? You can still submit to LDP/Ca$h Presents. Send in the first three chapters, written or typed, of your completed manuscript to:

LDP: Submissions Dept
Po Box 870494
Mesquite, Tx 75187

DO NOT send original manuscript. Must be a duplicate.

Provide your synopsis and a cover letter containing your full contact information.

Thanks for considering LDP and Ca$h Presents.

Chapter 1

Before I could even think about what I was doing, I was aiming the .40 out of the window, and placing my finger on the trigger. Wasn't nobody about to hurt my sister, I didn't give a fuck who Mikey was.

"Jahliya, get down!" Then I squeezed the handle of the gun, raised the front window and stuck my head out of it. "Say, Mikey! What the fuck you doing beating on my aunt's door like, you crazy? You got a problem or something?"

Mikey mugged me and moved one of his Goons out of the way. He stepped forward and got as close to the open window as he possibly could. "Mane, yo' sister got some shit that belongs to me. Tell her to return my shit, right now, or we're about to have a serious problem, know that homeboy."

"Look homie, I don't know what the fuck you think this is? But my sister ain't gotta take shit from you. You can kill all those idle ass threats, too. Ain't no ma'fucka finna put their hands on her, that shit ain't happenin'."

Mikey frowned and looked me over as if I wasn't shit. Two of the men behind him held up their full automatics and pointed them in my direction.

Mikey snickered. "Aw, so you think this shit is a game, huh, JaMichael? Nigga if I give the word, I'll have Veronica whole house blown off the ma'fuckin' map. This shit ain't no game to me, homeboy. Tell that bitch to bring me my muthafuckin' work. She got one minute or all you ma'fuckas in that house getting smoked." He cocked his gun and sucked his teeth as if he was the hardest nigga in the world.

I didn't like no ma'fucka making threats toward my sister. Jahliya was the love of my life. I didn't give a fuck what transpired this night, Mikey was gon' have to pay for calling my sister out of her name, and for having his homeboys point their weapons at me. I couldn't accept none of that shit.

"Say Potna, give me a second to holla at her. What's she supposed to have of yours anyway?"

"Nigga, that bitch know! Tell her to give you my shit. Time is ticking, my nigga. On everythang." He held his weapon against his shoulders.

"A'ight, I'ma fuck wit' you in a minute, hold on." I closed the window.

Jahliya had a purple Crown Royal bag full of jewelry on the bed. Half of the contents were spilled out. I saw three gold, iced Rolexes. Two iced bracelets, and five gold dripping chains.

"Where the fuck you get all of this from, Jahliya?"

"From his sucka ass. You see, that's the thing, Ja-Michael, I don't know what the fuck he's sweating me for. I don't know if it's for the kilos, or his three million dollars, worth of jewelry. All I know is that it can't be for both."

My head was spinning. "So, what do you wanna do?"

She shrugged. "I don't know, but I'm not giving this nigga both things. I know for a fact he's only here for one or the other. Go back to the window and ask him what I'm supposed to have. Feel that nigga out and see what's good."

"Damn, Jahliya, you got us in some bullshit. You shoulda told me before you was going to hit this nigga. Got this ma'fucka all in front of auntie crib acting a damn fool," I said, stepping out of the room, closing the door behind me. When I made it back to the front room, I opened the window and stuck my head out. "Mikey, tell me what she's supposed to have. I wanna get whatever she took from you back to you like asap."

"Mane tell that bitch to bring me my ice! Bring me my ice or feel these ma'fuckin' slugs. That's y'all last warning. Say mane, surround this ma'fuckin' house. If this bitch or this fuck nigga ain't gave me what belongs to me in the next few minutes, I want all clips emptied. That's on Duffle Bag," Mikey said, hitting his chest.

He was one of the bosses of the Duffle Bag Cartel. The Duffle Bag Cartel was one of the most money-making, flamboyant, flashy living, lethal Cartels in the city of Memphis. They operated out of the Black Haven housing projects, and those of the Orange Mound. Both stomping grounds were known for breeding fast money getting, cold-blooded killers.

Before I could say a word Jahliya handed me the Crown Royal bag that was stuffed with his jewelry. "Tell that punk ass nigga I wasn't gon' keep his shit. I just wanted to show him how reckless he was when it came to trusting bitches."

"Later for that." I opened the window and held the bag out to him. "Here man, she said she wasn't going to keep yo' jewels, bruh. She just wanted to show you how reckless you were when it came to trusting bitches. "

Mikey reached and yanked the bag out of my hand. "Gimme my shit!" He started searching through the bag, pulling his jewelry out piece by piece. When he saw that his jewelry was all there he nodded his head. "Tell that bitch to get her ass out here, right now. She gotta answer for her sins."

Ghost

Chapter 2

Jahliya tried for the third time to unsuccessfully move me out of her way. "Get out of my way, JaMichael. I ain't scared of him. He thinks because he got all them dudes with him. I'm supposed to be spooked? Yeah right!"

I pushed her lil' ass back on the bed. Mikey and his crew had moved to the backyard of Veronica's house, and Mikey was demanding that Jahliya come outside so he could speak with her face to face. I wasn't with that shit, I had already hit up Getty, and told him what the situation was. He assured me he was on his way. "Look, Jahliya, you need to calm yo lil' ass down. Not only are them niggas out there super deep, but they got guns. Them ma'fuckas could end our lives tonight."

She waved me off. "I don't give a fuck, ain't no ho in me, JaMichael. Those punks think just because they got guns that we're supposed to cower. I'd rather die standing up to them, then walk away like a coward. If they gon' kill me, they gon' have to do it. Now get the fuck out of my way." She jumped up and pushed me as hard as she could. I landed against the dresser, then she rushed out of the room, and through the back door of the house.

By the time I made it outside Mikey had Jahliya pinned against Veronica's apple tree by her throat. His goons stood around with their guns out. They were looking me over as if they were hoping I did something stupid. Mikey lifted Jahliya into the air.

"Bitch, you got the nerve to steal from me, huh? You thought you was fucking wit' one of them lame ass niggas a something?" he asked, choking her so hard she began to slap at his wrists.

I made a move in their direction, and his goons blocked my path by forming a barrier in front of them. The tall, dark-skinned, heavy-set one, stepped forward with a Tech in his hand. "Fuck nigga, you even think about crossing this here line, I'ma put this whole hunnit round clip in yo' ass wit' no remorse. Now that bitch done ripped off, my nigga. She gotta suffer the consequences. That's the way this shit finna go."

Mikey dropped Jahliya to the ground. She began coughing and holding her throat. She hacked, and spit on the ground, the whole time she was gasping for air. Mikey kicked her in the ass. "Punk ass, bitch."

I lost it and tried to break through the barrier. His guys threw me back. I fell to the ground and hopped right back up. Now my gun was aimed at Mikey. I was ready to blow his muthafuckin' head off his shoulders. There was the constant sound of guns cocking, then Mikey started laughing like a maniac.

Jahliya slowly climbed to her feet by use of the big Apple tree. The sun shined on her face, causing her to squint her eyes. "Fuck you, Mikey. You think you run this world? Nigga you ain't shit!" she snapped. "Kill his ass, Ja-Michael, blow his pussy ass away. Any man that beats on a woman doesn't deserve to live," she said this with tears running down her cheeks.

Now I was really crushed, I hated seeing my sister cry. Whenever she shed tears for some reason it caused me to become irate. "Mikey, let my sister go nigga. Then me and you can squash this shit, right here, right now."

All eyes were on me. Mikey muffed Jahliya as hard as he could, knocking her to the ground. Instead of her staying there, she jumped up with her fists balled.

"Come on, muthafucka. You wanna pick on me because I'm a woman? Come on, I ain't scared to die," she yelled.

"Fight me, Mikey. Fight me, and we can squash this shit. My sister is a female. Of, course you gon' be able to do all of that fuck shit to her. Now try yo' luck wit' me. Let's see how the cards change," I challenged. I was so heated my vision was going blurry. That only happened when I was at my angriest point.

"Drop that gun, JaMichael." He snatched up Jahliya and pressed his gun to the back of her head. "Drop that ma'fucka or I'ma knock her shit off."

"Fuck that, lil' bruh, shoot his ass. Splatter this nigga, and I'll see you on the other side." A lone tear ran down her cheek.

I saw Veronica appear in the window of her house, then she was gone just as quick as she appeared. I held the gun out so Mikey could see it. "A'ight man, take this ma'fucka. Just get that gun from the back of my sister's head."

He smiled and looked at me out the corners of his eyes. "Now you seem to be making sense, JaMichael." He stepped over to me and grabbed my gun with his left hand, then backhanded me with his right hand. I think my ego was hurt more than the slap I received.

I fell to one knee and felt the blood drip from my lip. I wiped it away and nodded my head. Yeah, I was gon have to body this nigga. I didn't know when, or how, but I knew if he didn't kill me, I was going to kill him sooner or later. Instead of staying on my knee like a punk, I stood tall. His Goons rushed me and hemmed me up against the fence.

Mikey grabbed Jahliya around the neck with his bicep and took to dragging her across the yard. "Say, JaMichael, you and this bitch owe me. Until I figure out just how much

I want you muthafuckas to pay for betraying me, Jahliya gon' be right wit' me." He continued to drag her across the backyard. She looked as if she were struggling to break free.

"What?" I started fighting his Goons, trying my best to break free of them. No matter what it seemed as if they were prepared for my mock escape attempt.

Somebody drove, Mikey's Range Rover around, and two masked dudes go out. I knew they were dudes because they had bulging biceps and were rocking black beaters. They snatched up Jahliya and stuffed her into the back of the truck before Mikey jumped in, and they pulled off.

I continued to struggle against Mikey's henchmen until I felt a hard blow to the back of my head. Everything went black. The next thing I knew I felt my face slam into the concrete, then I was snoring like a bear in hibernation.

***

Veronica woke me up twenty minutes later by slapping me lightly on the cheek. My eyes struggled to open. As soon as the sunlight penetrated my corneas I felt a pounding headache take over me. It felt so bad, I felt like throwing up.

"JaMichael, JaMichael, baby wakes up. Please, nephew, wake yo butt up."

I groaned in pain once again and sat up, frowning. I covered my eyes and shut my eyelids again. The grass felt itchy under me, and I swore it felt like something was crawling on me. Then my sister popped into my brain.

"Aw shit, Jahliya." I tried to get up.

As soon as I was on my feet, I felt dizzy and fell back on my ass. The world seemed to start spinning. Veronica was all over me trying to help me to stand back up.

"Danyelle! Danyelle! Get out here and help me get your cousin into the house!" she ordered.

Danyelle rushed into the backyard looking both ways as if she was paranoid. When she got to me, she kneeled down and helped me to my feet alongside Veronica. Together they guided me into the house, to the couch in the living room.

"Dang, his head is all busted up in the back. Look at it, mama." She held my head so Veronica could see my injury.

"Girl, I know what the back of his head looks like. I watched one of Mikey's shiesty ass guys buss him in the back of his dome with a gun. I'm just thankful didn't nobody shoot my baby." She kissed my cheek and rubbed the side of my face.

"Why did they do this to you and Jahliya, JaMichael? When are they going to bring, Jahliya, back?"

"Jahliya!" I yelled, jumping up, and rushing into my bedroom feeling woozy as hell.

My injuries caused me to forget the fact that my sister had been taken by Mikey and his Duffle Bag Cartel crew. I grabbed one of my Jordan shoeboxes and pulled a Glock .40 out of it. Then I loaded it with one of the magazines from the bottom of my dresser. Veronica came into the room as I was cocking it. Before she could even say a word, I was rushing past her, into the hallway where Danyelle blocked my path. I tried my best to step around her.

She sidestepped and got back in my way. "Cuz, you need to chill, damn. You ain't finna do shit but go out there with that one gun, and they gon wet yo ass up. Them niggas got all types of fully automatics over there."

Veronica came and stood in front of Danyelle. "Lil' girl watch yo' mouth. Don't you know I can hear you?" Then she turned to me with her back to Danyelle. "Listen, Ja-Michael, she's right, though. Mikey and his boys already know you're heated about your sister. They know you're coming to get her. You better believe they are ready for any attack you are about to try and pull on them. You have to be smart, or you're going to wind up in a body bag."

Danyelle shook her head and her face turned sad. "Yeah, and we don't want nothin' like that to happen to you. You're the only man we have in our lives, right now."

"Not only that, but it would be a stupid move," Veronica added. "You have to be smart any time you are going up against a whole mob of killas like them. You have to out-think them every step of the way. Your best play is to appear weak, and submissive. You need them, chumps, to let their guard down."

"*Weak and submissive*? Fuck that, ain't shit weak about me. And I ain't submitting to no nigga. If them Duffle Bag Cartel niggas don't let my sister go, I'm finna start bodying they ass one by one until they do. Mafuckas don't wanna play this game with me, I'm telling you. Jahliya is my heart of hearts. She's all I got." I was boiling hot, I was so mad I was shaking in rage. I couldn't believe Mikey's bitch ass would actually have the audacity to try some shit like this. "That's my fuckin sister!" I snapped, holding the gun against my side.

Danyelle walked up and rubbed my back. "We know cuz. We understand you're hurting. That's a given, but you can't be stupid, and you can't let this stuff break you. They ain't gon' keep her. She'll be home real soon, trust me on that." Danyelle wrapped her arm around my waist and attempted to lay her head on my shoulder.

16

I broke from under her and continued my path toward the front of the house. I felt like I had to do something. I felt offended and taken advantage of. I knew Jahliya was sure I would come for her. She knew I would come even if it would cost me my life.

Veronica sped down the hallway and grabbed my wrist. "Ghost, please baby. Please just listen to me. Maybe we should be smart and go to the police. We already know Mikey has her. We already know where their stomping grounds are. How hard would it be for us to go to the local authorities, and report what has taken place?"

"Yeah, JaMichael, that way you don't even have to get your hands dirty. I'm sure they'll lock all of their asses up for a hundred years. By the time they get out we would all be long gone, and on to greener pastures. What do you think?"

"*What do I think?*" I look from one to the other. "Are y'all fuckin serious, right now?" They both shifted uncomfortably. "Y'all want me to holler at Twelve. What the fuck do I look like? I ain't got that snitch shit in me. These niggas had the audacity to offend my sister. By offending her they have offended me. I ain't looking for no court justice, I'm looking for street justice. I'm about to go at them nigga's chin, that's all there is to it."

As soon as I finished my sentence Getty pulled up in front of Veronica's crib and blew his horn three times. By the time I got outside, he was making his way up to the porch with two guns in his hands. Veronica made one more mock attempt to stop me from going outside, but I yanked away from her and met Getty on the porch.

"What's good, my nigga?" he asked, with a red bandanna around his neck. His eyes were bloodshot. I could smell the liquor coming off his breath.

"That fuck nigga, Mikey, and a few of his Cartel members snatched up Jahliya a short while ago. I wanna track his bitch ass down and smoke him before I get my sister back."

Getty pulled his nose and scratched his arm. He rocked back, and forth on his toes. "Mane, you already know you're like my family. If you about to go and ruin a nigga's day, you already know I'm with you. All you gotta do is give me the time and place." He closed his eyes, and rocked back and forth on his toes again, before sniffing loudly, and clearing his throat.

I frowned. "Say Potna, you look like you rolling off that dope. You a'ight?"

Getty leaned against the railing of the porch and tucked both of his guns into his waistband. "I fucked around a lil' bit, but I'm good, though. Nigga, I'm more than capable of rolling behind you and handling this bidness. If these mogs wanna feel this steel, who am I not to give them what they asking for?" Whenever a nigga from Chicago used the term '*mog*' they basically meant the person they were referring to was a bitch or a fuck nigga. Getty was straight from the slums of Chicago, he used the terms Joe, and Mog a lot. Joe was just his way of calling a person Mane, or Potna.

"Well, let's roll for a minute. Let's ride through their hood and splash they ass like a wet T-shirt contest. Somebody gon' answer for, Jahliya." I was about to step down the porch steps when Veronica came running out of the house.

"JaMichael! JaMichael, take the phone. Jahliya is on the phone. Please hear her out before you do something stupid."

I turned around, grabbed the phone, and mugged her for a few seconds, then placed it to my ear. "Hello?"

Chapter 3

"Damn Joe, I can't believe we actually meeting up with these niggas instead of fanning they ass down. If it was up to me we'd go through that bitch and empty about four clips with no mercy. You're lucky I ain't in control," Getty said, taking a swallow from his bottle of Lean. He smelled just like the codeine. The scent was strong inside of the car.

"That shit would be stupid, Getty. This nigga got my sister. If we go through there on some Cowboys and Indians type shit, whether we fan down most of them niggas or not. All he gotta do is make Jahliya pay for my sins. I can't have that shit, it's my job to protect her. So, we finna meet him at this lil' meeting and see what's good. Once we get Jahliya back we can always come back and fuck his whole crew over. You already know I'm on that."

Getty looked me over from the passenger's seat and took another swallow from his drink before he threw the bottle out of the window. He ran his hand over his face and closed his eyes.

"Say, Joe, like I said before, I'm riding with you. However, you wanna handle shit, is cool with me. But on some real shit, I can't wait until we get on that bloody murderous shit. I'm most definitely on that. I ain't never liked them, niggas, no damn way."

"I know."

I rolled over some railroad tracks, then pulled into the old railway station off Pointer Street. After driving for two minutes the streetlights that illuminated the path that led to the viaduct on Pointer Place began to disappear. I drove onto the tracks and headed for the tunnel. I couldn't help but get an eerie feeling.

"Joe, we gotta be the stupidest niggas in the world. How the fuck do these niggas got us coming to the death railways at two in the morning to have a fuckin' meeting? Something ain't right, JaMichael. I know you can feel that in your gut," Getty said lighting a cigarette.

I could feel the sense of uneasiness he was obviously feeling, but I put it out of my mind. I had to get to Jahliya, and Mikey was the key to getting her back home, safe.

Even though all the meetings took place in Orange Mound, the ones that were really important, took place right at the old railway station on Pointer Place. Throughout the history of the projects, a lot of people had come up stankin' or gone missing in action in this area. I knew the history and I didn't give a fuck. I had to get Jahliya back by any means. If that meant there was a chance, I'd lose my life in the process, it was a risk I was willing to take for her.

"On some real shit, Getty. I don't give a fuck what I gotta do to get Jahliya back. I'ma do it, but I'm telling you bruh when I finally do get her back them Duffle Bag Cartel niggas gon' have hell to pay. That's my word."

Getty reached under his passenger seat and pulled up a Mach .90. He took a hundred round magazine from inside his coat pocket and slammed it inside of Mach, before cocking it. He looked over to me and smiled sinisterly. "JaMichael, I'm fucking wit' you, Joe. I'm ready to die for whatever you 'bout. Jahliya, like my sister, too, so let's get it." He bumped fists wit' me and adjusted his seat.

I kept rolling, the tracks kept the whip bouncing up and down. I drove inside the tunnel and followed the path until we wound up at a part of the station where there was a bunch of train cars. Mikey was waiting in front of the cars with what looked like twenty dudes. They were shirtless with guns in their hands. Mikey waited until I parked the whip before he stepped forward.

I got out of the car and slammed the door. I had two Glocks in my lower back and a .40 in my right hand. "What's good, Mikey?"

As soon as his Goons saw that I was armed they aimed their weapons at me as if they were ready to blow me away. I didn't give a fuck like I said before I was ready to die for my sister.

Mikey upped two 9mms that were equipped with red beams. He took the beams and pinned them on my fore-head. "You might as well put them guns down, right now, JaMichael. I'll have one of the lil' homies smoke yo' ass."

Getty stepped out of the whip with the Mach .90 and cleared his throat. "I'm letting you niggas know, right now, ain't nobody finna do shit to my nigga. You clowns ain't the only ones about that life." He tapped his trigger and enacted the red beam that was on top of his fully automatic. He scanned the entire crowd of Cartel members. "Act like y'all want this shit then."

Mikey took two steps back, he looked nervous. "Ja-Michael, you, betta tell that crazy ass nigga to put that bitch down. Anything happens to me, you can forget about see-ing Jahliya ever again. Don't forget her life is in my hands," he jacked with an evil smirk.

His words cut me deep, they both angered and irritated me. He had me by the balls as much as I hated to admit it. "Yo' Getty, lower that banger, bruh. We ain't come here on no bullshit. All we want is Jahliya back."

Getty sucked his teeth. "Nall, I'm good. You see I ain't stupid. I don't trust these coward ass niggas. The minute we lower these guns these niggas gon' try and pull some bullshit. He got his security armed and ready, and nigga you got yours. It's as simple as that."

Shid, I had to agree with the homie because he made perfect sense. "Say, Mikey, this what it is. The homie got a point. Long as you got your security on point, nigga, I got mine. Now where the fuck is my sister?"

A short heavyset dude stepped forward with plenty of tattoos all over his body. "Say, Potna, I don't know what y'all think dis is but y'all ain't running shit around here. I'm pretty sure we got more bullets in our clips than y'all do."

Getty placed his beam on his forehead. "Nigga that might be the case but all that mean is that we gon' have to kill as many of you bitches as we can before y'all have the chance to get off. I'm cool wit' that."

Mikey mugged me. "Yo' man's fronting. As far as what I'm being told, he ain't even got it in him to pull that trigger."

Getty leaned his head to the side and bit his bottom lip. "Oh, yeah?" He squeezed his trigger.

Boom! Boom! Boom!

The heavyset dude's head jerked backward, blood flew from the back, then he twisted in the air before he fell to the ground leaking. A puddle of blood formed around him.

My heart was beating faster than I ever remembered it beating. Two of my three guns were raised. I was expecting Mikey and his crew to get to bussing. In all honesty, I was praying silently that they didn't. I wasn't really prepared to be in an all-out shoot-out.

"A'ight, now you see my nigga won't hesitate to clap something. Let's stop with all of these games and get down to bidness. Where the fuck is my sister?"

Mikey stepped on the dead dude's body as if it were a doormat. Then he stepped into my face and looked me up and down. "JaMichael, you gon pay me for what your sister did. Until you do I'ma have her ass off the grid. You better pray you see her again."

"Fuck you say?" I snapped ready to body this nigga.

I noticed there was a full moon in the sky. It was dark as hell where we were posted on the railroad tracks. Our only light came from the headlights of my whip, and the other whips that were parked, and of course the moon.

"Nigga you heard exactly what I said. You owe me for what your sister did, and I intend on collecting. I think I'ma value that betrayal at a million dollars." He snickered.

"A million dollars? Nigga ain't no muthafucka finna give you a million dollars for shit. Fuck you think this is?" Getty snapped.

Mikey mugged him again. "Nigga, if he don't give me what the fuck I'm asking for, he gon' wind up finding lil pieces of his sister all over Memphis. This shit ain't no muthafuckin' game." He looked over at me. "So, what you gon' do JaMichael? You gon' hear me the fuck out, or you gon' kill your sister by your actions?"

I was so heated, I was starting to sweat. How dare this nigga ask me for a million dollars? I didn't have nowhere near that and didn't have the slightest idea how I was going to get it. "How the fuck you think I'm finna come up on a million dollars?"

"I don't know, and to be honest, I really don't give a fuck as long as you get me my cheese," Mikey said, looking over his shoulder at his homies.

"How long do I got to get you this money?" I asked defeated.

"Hell n'all, JaMichael! You ain't finna give this nigga no million dollars. We'll go to war with this nigga before I let that happen."

"Nigga, shut yo' ass up. Ain't no wars finna be jumping off. Y'all lil' niggas is peasants compared to me. This nigga right here is gon' get me my muthafuckin' money, that's gon' be that. I ain't got time to be playin' games with neither one of you pussies." He tucked his gun. "JaMichael, you gon' bring me a hunnit gees a week until you pay me off my money. If ever you should come up short something gon' happen to, Jahliya that you don't wanna know about. Now if you miss three payments, then its ashes to ashes for her ass, that's just that. Then if you suckas wanna go to war after all that, I ain't gon' have no problem taking y'all ass out the game with no remorse. Your first payment should take place a week from today, next Friday."

I was sick, but I knew I could come up on a hunnit gees a week if I really had to, and the way shit stood I really didn't have a choice.

"A'ight, I'll have yo' bread, Mikey. But when I pay you off how am I am going to get my sister back? How do I know you ain't finna be on no bullshit?"

He laughed. "You see, that's the thing, you don't know. All you can hope is that I'll be a man of my word. But if I was you, I wouldn't be late on either one of those payments. I mean you already know how fine, Jahliya is. She all strapped and shit. She be acting like she really don't wanna get down when a nigga know that lil' bitch is a low-key freak. To be honest with you, I'm hoping you fuck up so, me and the Cartel can have a little fun." He rubbed his hands together and ran his tongue over his lips.

As fast as lightning I closed the distance between us, and snatched him up by his fatigue jacket, slamming him

24

on my whip. "You bitch ass nigga, if you lay a finger on my sister, on my life I'ma take out everybody that shares your last name." His goons moved in closer with their guns on me.

Getty was scanning the crowd with his beam again. "Niggas, I dare anyone of you bitches to try me."

Mikey held up his hand. "Nall, don't shoot. This fuck nigga just mad, I got this." He smacked at my hand and bounced up. "Nigga, I said what I said. Have my money, or shit gon' get real ugly for y'all." He mugged me for a long time, then turned his back on me laughing like a maniac.

I stood in silence beside Getty long after Mikey and his crew pulled away.

Getty was still heated. "Man, we gotta handle that fool, JaMichael. Dawg done snatched up, Jahliya. You already know we can't let that shit ride. We gotta get our shit together for the sake of sis."

All I could do was nod, as the most sadistic shit of all my life continued to roam through my mind. "Bruh, you already know it's on. Let's ride out. Now we gotta handle them, and Grizzly." Life was getting serious.

Ghost

Chapter 4

Two days later, I sat with my head down beside Tamia in her bedroom while she tried to do her best to console me. "Damn, JaMichael, I really wish you would talk to me. Things would go a lot easier if you allowed somebody to enter your mind." She rested her head on my shoulder and sighed.

I couldn't get Jahliya off my brain. I was thinking about her every second of every hour. I was praying she was okay, and that Mikey hadn't put his filthy hands on her. I still hadn't made any moves toward getting the money Mikey was demanding. For some reason, I found myself way too stressed out that it was making it hard for me to focus.

"JaMichael, can you talk to me? Damn, baby, you need to understand I am here for you," she said softly.

I stood up. "That nigga said he wants me to pay him a million dollars to get Jahliya back. You saying you're here for me. A'ight tell me how much of this bread you're going to come up with then?" I challenged.

Tamia was silent, she continued to sit on the bed with her head down. After a while, her eyes slowly trailed up to me. "I don't know, JaMichael. I'm willing to do whatever it will take to make you happy. You already know, I don't know nothing about the streets like that, but if it's going to take me to hit the ground running just so I can have your back in the way I am supposed to, then so be it. All I want you to know is that you are not alone. The sooner you get that shit through your brain the better." Now she was up also and pacing the floor.

I didn't honestly know how her words were making me feel. I felt so broken because of the situation that Mikey had placed me and Jahliya in. I wanted to lash out at her. I wanted to pick a fight just so I could release some of the frustrations inside of me, but I didn't have it in me. Tamia wasn't my enemy, and I knew that. My beef was with Mikey and his Duffel Bag Cartel crew, along with Grizzly and his goons. Tamia was simply trying to do the best she could in support of me. I had to honor her for that.

I stepped into her path and held my arms wide open for her. "Come here, baby, I'm sorry."

She stopped and looked up at me, before placing her hand on her hip. "Say what?"

"I said I'm sorry, I didn't mean to be all disrespectful, and shit. I see what you're doing, I appreciate you. I already know how thoroughly you got my back. I just wanna say that means a lot to me."

Tamia slowly stepped into my arms and hugged me. "I swear to God, JaMichael, you're so damn bipolar. One minute you're snapping out on me about basically nothing. The next you're making me feel all special and stuff. I love you, baby, but you're driving me crazy." She hugged me tighter and rested her face on my chest.

"You should already know I'm stressing. Every time I imagine what them niggas could be doing to my sister it crushes my soul. I wasn't never supposed to let them get away with taking her. I'm her first, and last line of defense, and I failed her. I feel horrible, Tamia. This shit is killing me." I blinked and a tear fell from each one of my eyes.

I kept imagining Mikey doing some real horrible shit to my sister. I saw her crying, defenseless. I imagined her the way she looked as a little girl, instead of a grown woman. The more I saw that image of her the angrier it made me. Until I was in full tears, without the sobbing sounds, hugging Tamia as firm as I could.

She started crying. "JaMichael, I'm sorry, baby. I'm sorry your family has to go through this. I wish I could change the circumstances because it isn't fair, but I can't. But I'm willing to do whatever it takes to ride beside you. You are not in this fight alone." She took a step back out of my embrace and held my face with both of her hands. She stared into my eyes, and then kissed my lips and wrapped her arms around my neck. "I love you, JaMichael. It's okay, baby, I'm fighting with you."

I felt the tears drip off my chin and the softness of her lips against mine. The two feelings combined drove me absolutely insane for some reason. I was missing Jahliya like crazy, but I was thankful Tamia was there. I could barely think straight. I knew I needed something to help me take my mind off the seriousness of my situation if only for a short while.

I slid my hand down Tamia's back and cuffed her ass. She was wearing a pair of tight, blue jean denim shorts that were all up in her ass. Both cheeks were exposed, and I didn't have no problem squeezing 'em.

"Tamia, I need some of this pussy, baby girl. I need something to take my mind off this bullshit with Mikey, and his crew." My fingers slid through her leg holes until I was rubbing her bald sex lips. They were hot and plump, I sucked on her neck, and led her up against the wall.

"Uh, Daddy, I don't know what time my mama gon' be home," she moaned.

I unbuttoned her jeans in the front and slid my hand down them. My middle digit entered her tight sheath, then it was going in and out of her. "Uh...uh...uh, Daddy, please."

"I need some of this pussy, baby. Daddy needs you," I urged.

She lifted her thick thigh and rested it on the side of my waist. Now I could really finger her at full speed. She was so tight, and that coochie was so fresh my finger could barely run in and out without having difficulty. She was also oozing like crazy. I couldn't help stopping and sucking that finger into my mouth.

"Stop…stop, Daddy. You gon get us caught!"

I finished sucking my fingers, picked her up and dropped her on the bed. I took her knees and forced them to her chest. That bussed her lil pussy wide open. It looked so good and ripe. There was a clear fluid that decorated the lips that made that shit sexy to me. I covered her box with my mouth and ran my tongue up and down her groove. Her meat tasted salty, and oh so good.

"Uuhhh, JaMichael! Daddy, that feels so good." She held her knees and opened her legs further. I slipped two fingers into her and worked them at full speed while I sucked on her erect clit. She humped into my face and started shaking like crazy. "Daddy…Daddy, ohhh shit! I'm cumming…I'm cumming!" She humped into me one hard time and squirted all over my face.

That shit drove me crazy, I started really licking and slurping while she screamed and flipped all over the bed. My fingers were a blur inside her. Finally, after she came two times back to back, I kneeled on the bed stroking my piece. It didn't take her long to catch on. She grabbed it out of my hand and sucked the head into her mouth. She trailed circles around it with her tongue. The next thing I knew, I was laying on my back while her head bounced up and down in my lap. Every so often her teeth would lightly graze the rim of my pipe, that drove me nuts. When I came, she held me as best she could in her lil' fist, pumping me up and down while she swallowed my seed, then licked up and down my shaft.

She stood on the side of the bed sucking her fingers. "Did you like that, Daddy? Do you think you're ready for some of this?" She held her brown lips apart and flashed me her pink.

My dick started jumping up and down excitedly. I grabbed her lil' ass and pulled her on top of me. She straddled me, reached under her and took a hold of my shaft, then slowly slid down it.

"Mmm, shit, Daddy!" It took a few seconds, but finally, she sank the majority of the way down it. She leaned forward and kissed my lips. "I love you so much, JaMichael."

I gripped that ass and rubbed it, before I was clenching her waist, pulling her down the rest of the way. Her pussy was overheated. She swallowed me with a tight fit, moaning into my neck.

"I love you, too, boo! Now ride, Daddy, ride me like you crazy about me."

She sat up straight and placed her hands on my chest. Then she started riding me with her head tilted backward. I could hear the sounds of our lovemaking coming from between her thighs. It sounded like wet sucking. It felt so good she had me groaning like a bitch. She held the headboard and bounced faster and faster. I pulled her tank top over her head and exposed her B cup titties. Her nipples were swollen from the mounds. They looked good, I started sucking them one at a time while she rode me. That turned her into an animal on top of me.

I bussed once and flipped her ass on her stomach. Then started dogging her out holding her waist. She cocked her right knee to her rib cage and took the dick like a true champion until I bussed again. This time I collapsed on top of her and sucked on the back of her neck. While my piece continued to throb inside of her body. We fucked for two hours straight and fell out.

***

About three hours later, we were awoken by Tammy, Tamia's mother, yanking the sheet off us. "Bitch, if you don't get yo' fast ass up and explain what the fuck you been doing? I'ma about to kill you and his grown ass!" She threatened, holding my Glock .40 in her hand.

Tamia jumped up beside me and tried to cover her private parts with her hand. "Mama, oh my God. I'm so sorry, I didn't know that you would be home this fast. I—"

Tammy swung and slapped the shit out of Tamia. Tamia fell to her knees holding her face. "Bitch, you got some muthafuckin nerve. You got this nigga all in my house while I'm at work. Y'all got my whole house smelling like dick and pussy." She mugged Tamia, then me.

I was standing there frozen, I didn't even bother covering myself. I saw her eyes trail down to my dick more than once. I didn't even care. "Look, Ms. Tammy, this ain't her fault. I was going through something, and I needed my baby. She tried to tell me that shit wasn't a good idea, but I was hardheaded. If you gon' whoop anybody's ass it should be mine," I confessed.

Tamia jumped up and ran out of the room. "You're always putting your hands on me. I'm so tired of this shit!" she yelled, as she ran past.

Tammy swung and missed her. "Bitch, then get the fuck out of my house! And you—" She pointed the gun at me and turned it around so only the handled was brandished. "You take this gun and get the fuck out of my house. Next time you need somebody to fuck, go find somebody else's fast ass daughter. You hear me?" she asked tossing the gun to me.

She glanced down at my dick again. This time she looked longer than she had before. Her nipples were poking through her blouse whereas they hadn't been before, I found that odd.

I took my gun and tossed it on the bed. "Like I said before, Ms. Tammy, I apologize. I didn't mean no disrespect, I just needed her. Matter fact, wait a minute." I picked up my pants off the floor and pulled out a knot of hundred-dollar bills. Then peeled off a gee and handed it to her even though I knew she wasn't going to take it.

She snatched it out of my hand and thumbed through it. "Ah, so you're a lil' baller, huh? You trying to buy my silence?" she asked looking me up and down. She turned around, closed the door, locked it and stepped back into my face.

The scent of her perfume made my dick hard all over again. It rose and poked her thigh, she didn't say a word. Because of her silence, I stepped forward and pressed him further into her.

"That money is just to show you your daughter ain't fuckin' wit' no bum ass nigga. I love her, and I'm down to hold her down. I see all you do is work—work—work. You ain't gotta be out there slaving the way you are. All you gotta do is tell me what you need. I'll make sure you got it, out of love for, Tamia."

Tammy frowned and rested her hand on my shoulder. Then she rubbed my chest. "I see you're all grown up now huh, JaMichael? You're old enough to pay bills and all that shit now?" Her hand went down and clutched my dick. She squeezed it and stroked it a few times too many. My knees got weak as a muthafucka.

"Like I said, all you gotta do is tell me what you need for this household. In honor of, Tamia, I'ma make sure you got it."

She squeezed it harder and looked into my eyes. "So, you gon' make that happen for, Tamia, huh? What about her, Mama? What are you going to do for me?" She kissed my neck.

Now my dick was really jumping. Tammy was a fine ass older woman. She looked just like her daughter, but her breasts were slightly larger, and her body just seemed more gorgeous to me. I already had a crazy thing for older women anyway. I preferred them and didn't know why. Maybe it was because I had mommy issues because I never knew my mother Blaze. Or maybe it was just because of all the covert shit Veronica used to do to me while I was a kid. Either way, Tammy was sexy as hell, and I was thirsty to know what her walls felt like.

"What do you want?"

She giggled. "JaMichael, you don't ever see a man around here do you?"

I shook my head. "Nall, what's that supposed to mean?"

"You should already know what I'm trying to do then." She pulled my piece and made me poke her directly in the center of her thigh gap. Since she was wearing a pair of thin pants I could feel her heat radiating through the material. "So, what you wanna do?" she asked licking along the length of my neck.

I couldn't believe how trifling she was acting. What type of female was down to fuck her daughter's boyfriend right after she caught them in the bed together? I didn't know, and before I could answer she kneeled on her knees.

Tamia started beating on the door. "Mama, open this damn door! Don't be snapping out on my man. He ain't your child!" she yelled pounding against the wood.

Tammy planted a kiss on the tip of my pole's head and stood up. "I'm gon' get me some of this young meat, just you watch. I ain't never seen no boy hung like you, Ja-Michael. You don' probably ruined my baby."

I didn't even know what to say to that. All I knew was that my dick was harder than calculus. Before she opened the door for Tamia, I was dressed, and feeling more guilty than a crook caught on camera.

Ghost

Chapter 5

"Nigga we at eighty-five gees. We got fifteen more thousand to make before we gotta meet up with this dude and drop him off all the hard-earned cash we done made over the last few days. I still can't believe we're allowing this fuck nigga to squeeze us like this. I say we start picking them niggas off one by one, sooner or later we'll find out where Jahliya is being held, and how to get her back," Getty said, before taking a long swallow from his bottle of Hennessey. He wiped his mouth, and flopped back down on the couch, taking the blunt from behind his ear, sparking it.

I sat across from him blowing my second blunt of Loud. I was high as a kite, and missing Jahliya worse than a little kid dropped off at daycare by his mother. I felt sick, and my eating habits were horrible. I was down to one petty ass meal a day. That meal mostly consisted of a bag of chips, maybe a piece of chicken if I was real hungry. I was losing weight, and I could see it every time I looked in the mirror.

"Nigga, I don' already told yo' ass we gotta be smart for now. I got some shit in rotation. When it pulls through we gon' be able to get at them nigga's chin like true Orange Mound killas. Ain't nobody about to abuse, Jahliya, and get away with that shit. Over my dead body. You feel me?" I took three hard pulls and inhaled. I closed my eyes and allowed the weed to take over my senses. "What's good with that other move, though?"

"You talking about that shit with, Grizzly? Everything's in motion. We gon' holler at two of his cousins later tonight. I found out he moved his duck off again. Supposedly his two cousins he brought down with him are his top security personnel. These niggas finna be laid up with a few

Black Haven strippers, pieces my baby mama put in place. We gon let they ass get sucked, and fucked, then we gon' run through that bitch and inflict some real pain until they give us the information we need."

"That sounds like a plan to me," I said, dumping the ashes from my blunt into the ashtray, and taking another pull. "Keeping that shit real—" I took the time to blow the smoke toward the ceiling of Getty's mother's basement. "I gotta get this killer urge out of me. Ever since this shit happened to my sister, I ain't had the chance to body shit. I'm starting to become frustrated. I gotta watch a nigga soul escape his body, Getty. I know that shit sounds crazy as fuck, but it's the truth." I took four more pulls, and inhaled, holding the smoke in until I could feel the burn.

Getty shook his head. "Bruh, that shit don't sound crazy to me. Shid, I feel the same way. Ain't no therapy like icing a nigga. Murder heals all wounds, I truly believe that."

As soon as he said this, his baby mama Candy came down the stairs holding a plate of food. Candy was darkskinned, thick, with natural light brown eyes, and her hair was cut in a short style. "Here, Getty, you, betta eat all of this, too. You told me you was hungry. I definitely didn't feel like cooking." She looked past him to me. "Ghost, are you hungry?" She smiled and seemed to bat her fake eyelashes at me.

I shook my head. "Nall, I'm good, Candy. Thank you for asking, though."

She shrugged her shoulders. "Oh, it ain't no problem." She sucked on her bottom lip and looked sexy, I couldn't even deny that fact.

Getty grabbed his plate and smacked Candy on her ass. Her cheeks jiggled for a split second, then stopped. I imagined what it would feel like to fuck her from the back, and my shit started to rise. I had to shake myself out of my zone.

"Stop Getty, damn." She looked over at me. "You know I ain't fuckin' wit' you like that no more. Damn, don't get shit twisted." She started making her way back up the stairs and stopped midway up. "If I don't see you before you leave, Ghost, you have a good night, and be safe out there."

"You have a good night, too, Candy. I'll catch you another time," I returned.

"Hopefully," she flirted.

I watched her go back up the stairs with her shorts all in her black ass cheeks. Damn, she was thick. That's all I kept thinking about.

When she was out of sight, Getty waved her off. "Punk ass bitch be getting on my nerves, Joe. I wish I never got that bitch pregnant," he snapped.

"Why you say that?" I asked, praying my piece would go down. I kept seeing images of Candy's ass in my mind, it was driving me up the wall.

"Shorty just toxic as hell. She always on that drama shit, and whenever I don't give that bitch whatever it is she's asking for she got a habit of trying to keep me away from my daughter. That shit so weak to me. That's why I don't be hitting her hand with shit extra outside of that child support. If she can't make it on that then she can open them thighs, and just maybe she can catch a couple of bills, but that's it."

I was disgusted with Getty for even saying some shit like that. He musta saw the look on my face because he waved me off. "Bruh, you do know that that child support shit barely covers a week's worth of expenses, right?"

I knew that because before my father Taurus got his child support suspended because he was incarcerated, Veronica used to always complain about how little the bread the government was ordering him to pay helped her with the bills for me and Jahliya. As I got older I started to understand that firsthand.

"Bruh, I don't give no fuck. Fuck that bitch. That's all she getting from me if she ain't letting me fuck on a regular," he jacked.

"And that's why I don't fuck wit' yo' trifling ass on that level, right now. I been doing this shit basically on my own anyway. Real women find out how to take care of theirs, so kiss my ass, Getty!" she yelled, and slammed the upstairs door.

"Bitch, that's your problem. You're always in my muthafuckin' bidness, get a life!" He turned to me and downed the rest of his Hennessey. "Bruh, let's get the fuck out of this bitch before I catch a case."

I nodded. Getty led the way back upstairs. When you come out of the basement the first room of the house you step into is the kitchen. Candy was at the stove making a paper plate full of food. For some reason the refrigerator was open, and I saw that it was damn near empty, with the exception of a few items, and a box of baking soda. I could see Carmen, Getty's three-year-old daughter sitting at the kitchen table, I imagined prepared to eat. Getty walked into the room, picked her up from her seat, and kissed all over her.

While he was out of earshot I guess my conscious got the better of me. "Say, Candy, I know shit hard trying to raise that baby girl on your own. Even though it ain't my bidness, huh." I handed her a roll of hundreds totaling five thousand dollars. I knew it would set me back for the total

I needed to come up with for Mikey, but I hated to see a single mother struggling. I felt like I had to do something.

Candy looked over the knot and exhaled. "Damn, Ghost, this ain't gon' do nothin' but make shit worst for us."

I didn't understand what she was talking about. "What do you mean?"

"Man, I know you can tell how much I'm feeling yo' fine ass? And have been ever since the ninth grade before, Getty even came into the picture. I mean I ain't going into it because that ain't smart, but just know you been on my radar." She kissed me on the cheek and continued to make what I assumed her daughter's plate. "Thank you, too."

"Anythang you need, don't hesitate to get at me."

"I won't," she promised, smiling.

I couldn't help but glance down at those sexy thighs again. She was so well put together. I had to get the fuck out of that kitchen because she had me feeling some type of way.

***

Getty drove his Ford Explorer with a Tech-9 on his lap. The clip hung out of the handle like a Pez dispenser. He had half of his face covered with a ski mask and dark shades on his face. I could tell something was bothering him because he kept mumbling to himself, then he would nod his head.

Finally, after us rolling for about fifteen minutes with no words exchanged, I got irritated. "Yo' nigga, what the fuck is good with you?"

He ignored me for damn near a full minute. Then he looked over at me and grunted. When he pulled the truck to the stoplights, he pulled on his nose and sniffed hard. "I can tell, Candy feeling you, JaMichael."

"What?" I asked, trying to play the fool.

"Yeah, nigga, that bitch was eyeing you every chance she got. She always every time you come through, too. I don't even think she was going to open the door until she pulled the curtain to the front window back and saw me with you." He shook his head. "Life is a bitch."

"Bruh, you already know I would never fuck wit' yo' baby mama on that level. That shit would be ultimately trifling. A nigga would have to be rotten to the core."

He shrugged his shoulders. "Fuck that bitch, she grown as hell. If she wanna give you some pussy then smash her ass. I ain't tripping. All I care about is my daughter. I ain't never loved no bitch, my nigga." The light flicked green. He pulled off and got into traffic.

Even though these were the words that came out of Getty's mouth, I could tell he was feeling some type of way. He still cared about Candy. I could tell because any time she shot his ass down his mood always changed to that of a depressed one.

"Well, I don't give a fuck if you cared if I smashed her or not, that's a line I could never cross. You're my nigga, it's too many hoes out here for me to be fuckin' yo' baby mama."

"Nigga, I guess. You can do what you wanna do. I'm just letting you know I can tell Candy feeling you. She wanna give you some pussy. Y'all both grown, that's just that. If Tamia wanted to give me some pussy nigga, I'd be all—" He stopped midsentence and looked into his rearview mirror. "Nigga, this same ass jeep been following us for about five minutes now. What the fuck they on?"

I turned around in my seat and looked out of the back window. There was a black Jeep Wrangler with Mississippi plates, and tinted windows lurking behind our truck. "That ma'fucka been following us fa real?" I took my Tech-9 and cocked that bitch.

Getty nodded. "Hell, yeah, but watch this though. I'm finna roll through this arboretum up on Jackson and see if they follow. If they do, I got a trick for they ass." He continued to roll and kept glancing in his rearview mirror with a mug on his face. "Yeah, I got a trick for these niggas."

He pulled into the arboretum, and sure enough, the Jeep waited, then pulled in behind us trying its best to keep a safe distance. I was geeked. I knew right then we were being hunted.

"Getty, hit the gas a lil' bit and let me out up there." I pointed where the road began to turn and break off into two separate directions.

"What? Nall, nigga, I got something even better."

"Fuck that, I wanna smoke every nigga that's up in that bitch. I'm tired of is playing the victim." I slid on my black leather gloves. I could feel my heart pounding in my chest.

"Nigga, a'ight, but if you handle these clowns then I get to handle the ones we gotta take care of tonight. Deal?" he asked, looking over at me.

"We'll cross that bridge when we come to it." I returned ready to wet up some shit.

Getty laughed and sped up the truck. He created a nice distance before he slowed down just enough for me to jump out. The lake was right behind me. I could smell the scent of the seaweed, and hear the Crickets chirping. Getty pulled the truck away from me and continued to drive forward. All I could see was his brake lights after a while. It was pitch black all around, with the exception of an occasional lightning bug that flashed through the air. I jogged along the brush and snuggled into some bushes that were just to the side of the road.

I took a deep breath and waited. The weapon felt heavy in my hands. As I looked into my left I could see the Jeep creeping slowly along. I waited until it was close enough for me to do my thing before I ran into the center of the road fearless.

Chapter 6

Boom! Boom! Boom! Boom! The tech-9 spit and shattered their windshield.

The Jeep swerved and sped off the road crashing into a bush. I was on their ass, bussing my Tech, chopping that bitch down with no remorse.

Boom! Boom! Boom! Boom! The fire from the Tech-9 was bright in the night.

I heard more of their windows explode. I rushed the vehicle and kicked in the remainder of the windshield. The driver laid slumped against the driver's door. His eyes were closed, and his mouth was wide open. The horn airbag was deployed. Before I could get a good look into the passenger's seat or the back of the whip shots were fired at me from the rear.

Bloom! Bloom! Bloom! Bloom!

I damn near busted my shit falling backward trying to get out of the line of gunfire. I could hear the bullets whipping past my head. Then I was bussing my gun again.

Boom! Boom! Boom! Boom! More shots were returned by the occupants inside the truck.

The interior lit up with shot after shot. I kept getting the uneasy feeling I was seconds away from being hit. They sounded as if they were popping a 9mm or a handgun of some sort. Getty came storming down the road. He slammed on the breaks and jumped out of his whip on bidness. He aimed his Tech and went right to work, chopping their Jeep with shot after shot. I heard somebody on the inside holler, then five shots came from inside of the jeep before me and Getty spent our entire clips wetting up the occupants on the inside of it. When it was all said and done, we dragged the three to the middle of the road and looked them over.

Getty pulled their masks off. "Damn, JaMichael, do you recognize anyone of these niggas?"

I could barely see them in the dark, but the headlights from Getty's truck helped a little bit. "Nall, I ain't never seen either one of these dudes before. Let's get the fuck up out of here before somebody roll-up." I hopped over one of their bodies and jumped into his passenger seat.

He stayed back and looked them over for a short while before I hopped into the driver's seat. "That's fucked up when you're beefing with so many niggas that we don't even know. Who sent these chumps to kill our ass? These ma'fuckas was armed and ready for war. Somebody had to put them on to us," he said and rolled over each of their leaking bodies. "We gotta conquer this game, JaMichael. We gotta conquer this bitch quick, or we gon be the next ma'fuckas laid out slumped in the streets."

I didn't give a fuck what cards was dealt to me, I felt like I would always find a way to prevail and come out with my life. That street shit wasn't just on me, it was written across my heart. I knew sooner or later I would become a king of the slums. "Fuck them, niggas. Let's go and handle this other bidness."

"Now you speaking my language," Getty said, stepping on the gas.

***

About forty-five minutes later, Getty rolled into a garage and cut the engine. He pulled the half mask off his face and took an all-black ski mask from the center console and pulled it over his head.

"Katey, finna meet us at the side door and let us in. Apparently, one of the niggas that we're about to get down on is her sister's baby daddy. She says that nigga is from Black Haven, and he is as shiesty as they come. Shorty can't wait until we get rid of his ass."

All that was fine and dandy, but I had a problem with somebody else being a part of this move we were about to buss. I wasn't trying to put my freedom at risk for nobody. "Bruh, who the fuck is this bitch, and why she knows so much about what we finna do?" I asked, sliding my ski mask over my head.

Getty looked over at me at the same time he started to reload his Tech. "Dis bitch cool, JaMichael. I been fucking wit' her for a lil' while now. I can trust her."

"Fuck you say?" I snapped, slamming a fifty-round clip into my Tech-9.

"I said I can trust her. We don't got shit to worry about. In fact, she's the one who's setting these niggas up for us. If it wasn't for her we'd still be back at square one with that nigga Grizzly hunting us down, instead of us coming for him just as lethal. So, in a way we owe, Katey." He checked his surroundings, then looked back over to me.

From the rearview mirror, I could see the alley that was behind us. A stray black cat ran across my vision and disappeared. "I don't owe this bitch shit, and I'm letting you know, right now nigga, I ain't about to let this bitch keep breathing knowing what we're about to go in here and do. Only a fool would let that happen."

Getty was quiet for a second. "Joe, ain't no way in hell I'ma about to let you do that to her, JaMichael. You just gon' have to trust me on this." He looked behind his back again, and out the window.

I saw a figure move from the rearview mirror, and then a person was coming into the garage with a black hood over their head. Before I could even think about it, I pushed open the passenger's door and fell to the ground with my Tech raised, aiming. "Getty, get yo' ass down, bruh! It's a hit!"

"Nooooooo, JaMichael, don't shoot! That's my bitch!" Getty hollered, jumping out of the truck behind me.

The figure froze and threw her arms up. The hood fell off her head and exposed the fact that she was a Spanish female. Both of them was lucky my shit had been clicked on safety because I had to reload it because had it not been I would have lit her ass up with bullet after bullet because of the way I was trying to squeeze the Tech's trigger.

Getty ran and jumped in front of her. He waited for the situation to become still, then he snapped, "Damn, nigga, you almost kilt my bitch. Can't you see she pregnant?" He pulled open her trench coat and exposed her baby bump. She looked as if she were every bit of four months pregnant.

I got up from the ground and mugged both of them. "She lucky my shit was on safety, Getty. On my mama in heaven, had my shit been live, I would have put at least twenty holes in her ass. Fuck was you doing creeping like that, Katey?"

Katey took a step behind Getty and shrugged her shoulders. She couldn't have been any older than seventeen. "Getty texted me and told me to meet him in this garage, right now. I was just doing what he told me to do."

"Yeah, nigga, she good. You just gotta calm yo' trigger happy ass down." He frowned and pulled her into his embrace. "Bitch, you good?" She nodded. "My shorty good?"

Once again, she nodded, but this time she placed her hand on top of her belly and began rubbing it. "He's good,

Papi. Listen, Junior, and his three homeboys are up there bagging Grizzly's work. They just started so they are set to be there for a minute. I told him I was about to run to the Gyro shack a couple of blocks over because I was having some crazy cravings. None of them fools volunteered to go for me. They just let me leave which is a good thing. Because of the amount of work they were bagging up, I was expecting them to ask me a million questions, but they didn't, and that's a good thing."

Getty pulled her under his arm. "That's what's up. We about to go up here and handle bidness. When we finish you better be ready to smile in your sisters face like you don't know what happened to her nigga. I mean you better be ready to console her and everything."

"Papi, you talking like this is my first rodeo. Well, it ain't, I know what I gotta do. I'ma be right here when you make it back downstairs. Y'all just go in there and handle your bidness." She kissed his cheek and sat in the passenger's seat of the whip.

I didn't like nothing that had transpired. I didn't know where this broad had come from. I didn't know if she could keep her mouth shut, and I didn't want to roll the dice on her either. As much as all of this rubbed me the wrong way I had to trust Getty. I didn't think my Potna would misjudge anybody, plus he wanted to get at Grizzly and his entire operation for what they had done to his people.

Getty opened the door to the truck and grabbed the house keys from Katey. Then we were out, and making our way across the backyard on bidness, with me behind him second-guessing this bitch's place in our lick. When we got to the back door, Getty slid the key into the lock and pushed the door inward. It opened to a dark hallway. He looked back at me and nodded.

There was a full moon in the clear sky, along with a bunch of stars. It felt like it was every bit of ninety degrees, with a gentle breeze. That was the only thing gentle about this night because everything that was going on inside of me was aggressive. Instead of me waiting for Getty to creep up the steps as if we were cat burglars or some shit. I rushed ahead and slipped into the first floor's door that was wide open. As soon as I stepped inside I could smell the stench of cigarette smoke and beer. That shit turned my stomach like eating something that didn't agree with me. The house was filthy. There was trash all over the place, and big ass roaches that crawled all over the floor. To my right in the next room was a blue light. I could hear voices, and I knew it was where Grizzly's men were bagging up his work.

Getty rushed and placed his hand on my shoulder. He talked directly into my ear, "Nigga remember we gotta find out where this nigga laying his head. We can hit these clowns, but we gotta get that information first."

I nodded and brushed past him. I took the lead and rushed into the dining room where they were bagging up three bricks of Tar, upped my Tech, and slammed it to the back of Junior's head, snatching him from the chair.

"Fuck nigga get yo' ass up, you already know what time it is." He tried to struggle against me, until I flung him to the floor, and pressed my Airmax on his throat.

Before the other two niggas could make a move, Getty rushed into the room trigger happy.

Boom! Boom! Boom! His bullets chopped into the first dude's chest and slammed him against the wall. He slid down it bloody and wound up slumped forward, with his head in his lap.

The other one backed up and tried to grab a handgun from his pants. By the time he got it out, my Tech was spitting on him as if he were a baseball field. He landed on top of the table, breaking it. His brains leaking out of his face, spilling on to the carpet.

Getty kicked him in the side and started stripping him. "Say, Mane, find out where that fuck nigga, Grizzly, laying his head."

Junior tried to get up again. I raised my foot as high as I could and brought it back down in the middle of his chest as hard as I could. He rolled on his side, coughing up yellow shit.

"Fuck Grizzly at nigga?"

Junior continued to cough, his dark-skinned face turned a shade of purple. "Hold up—" More coughing. "Hold the fuck up." He scooted back on his ass.

"Hold up?" I pressed the Tech to his shoulder and pulled the trigger. *Boom!* He flew backward, hollering like a woman in labor. "Nigga, you don't tell me to hold on. Where the fuck is Grizzly laying his head?"

He squeezed his shoulder, blood spilled out of him and oozed down his fingers. "He stays in Latham Village. He got a townhouse over there. Whatever y'all got going on with him ain't got shit to do wit' me," he groaned.

Getty kicked him in the head and left him dizzy. "We need an address?"

He began hollering at the top of his lungs. He struggled to get up. "Please man, don't do this shit to me! That nigga got fifty gees here, and three bricks of that Mexico City raw that he about to pick up first thing in the morning! If I give y'all all of it would y'all spare my life? I don't want no parts of this shit," he reiterated.

Getty nodded. "Hell, yeah, nigga if you break bread we'll let yo' ass live, and make sure you walk away from this situation with only the injuries you've suffered this far," Getty promised.

I wasn't agreeing to that, I was still on the fence about letting this bitch live that so-called had his seed.

"A'ight then, look, all the money is wrapped up in a blanket, and in the closet in that middle room right there. Y'all take that shit. The bricks is on the table, and just let me keep my life. Y'all already popped me up. Broke a few ribs and busted my face."

"Nigga that room, right there?" I pointed.

He nodded.

Getty rushed into it and started rummaging around it. I kept my Tech pinned on Junior. He was fucked up with blood streaking down his face. He held his shoulder and continued to wince in pain.

"Please let me go man. Please, fuck, Grizzly! That nigga don't give a fuck about nobody but himself."

Getty rushed back into the room. "I got that shit, bruh, I got it. This ma'fucka full of cash."

"Oh, it is?" I stood over Junior. "Good looking nigga." *Boom! Boom! Boom! Boom!*

Getty put three in him just so he could feel like I didn't handle everything on my own, then we were grabbing the bricks, throwing them in the garbage bag with the money, and running up out of there. When we got back to the garage, I was expecting Katey to be waiting on us, but she was nowhere in sight. That alone sent my paranoia through the roof.

Getty played it off as if he wasn't worried. He simply got behind the driver's wheel and pulled out of the garage. Since he didn't say nothing about his pregnant bitch being missing in action I didn't say nothing either, but I was as nervous as a smuggler getting pulled over by the cops. I didn't know his broad, and I most definitely didn't trust her. Anybody that would set up their sister's baby father had to be grimy.

Ghost

Chapter 7

Bubbie hit me up the next morning. "JaMichael, bring yo' ass outside. I wanna spend some time with you today. I ain't trying to take no for an answer either. That's why I'm waiting right outside," she said into the phone.

I was sleepy as hell, and I'd been dreaming about Jahliya. The dream was so vivid it actually felt like I was with her. I held my phone to my ear with my eyes closed. "Give me like a half an hour to get ready, I'm just waking up."

"A'ight, JaMichael, don't be on no bullshit. Don't have my ass out here waiting for a million years. If you laid up with some bitch tell that ho to kick rocks. You fuckin' wit' yo' pregnant baby mother for the day." She hung up the phone before I could even respond.

As soon as I hung up the phone with her, Danyelle knocked on the door twice, then pushed it inward. She stepped into my room with a pair of tight ass boy shorts that were all up in her gap. Her sex lips were molded to the material. Above the boy shorts was a half-cut pink shirt that matched the color of her shorts.

"Dang, Ghost, what you trying to do, sleep all day?" She closed the door and popped back on her legs.

I sat up and stretched my arms above my head. "What you doing in my room, Danyelle? You already know yo' lil' ass is in jeopardy around me," I said standing up. Since I had just woke up my piece was semi-hard. I peeped how she locked her eyes on it, right away.

She sucked on her bottom lip and smiled so sexy like. "You know my mama ain't here, right now, right?" She came across the room and rubbed my boner.

She squeezed it and slid her hand between her own thighs. I watched how her middle finger separated her sex lips through the material. I would be lying if I said Danyelle didn't have one of the fattest pussies I'd ever seen in my entire life.

"Shawty you, betta let my shit go before you get yourself in trouble."

She licked her lips, and dropped down to her knees, then pulled me out of my boxers, and sucked me into her mouth three times before she released me. "I might be young but I'm ready, JaMichael. This forbidden shit makes my coochie wet. I love this family, shit, I can't help it." She licked around the head, and sucked me twenty straight times, before pulling me out.

My pole was shiny with her spit and my toes were curled. My breathing was rugged, and my dick was harder than a bully on the schoolyard. She planted light kisses over the head, before sucking me like a pro. The noises she made started driving me nuts. She stroked me with her right hand and rubbed her own pussy with her left.

She popped me out again. "I need you to fuck me, Ja-Michael. Take my virginity, I ain't trying to lose my virginity to nobody but you. It gotta be our bloodline." She kept stroking me while she was saying this shit.

I wound up on the bed, on my back with her lying beside me stroking my dick at full speed. Every now and then, she would stop, and suck on it for two minutes straight. She put her leg up while she was lying on her side and pulled down her panties.

She popped me out of her mouth once more. "Look at my pussy, JaMichael. It's fresh, you gotta be the first one to get some of this, it has to be you. I'm so hot down there."

I could hear my phone buzzing, I knew it was Bubbie blowing me up. I had gone well past thirty minutes. It had been damn near forty-five, and I wasn't nowhere near ready to come outside. Danyelle jumped on top of me and straddle my waist. She sucked on my neck and ground her pussy into my piece. I grabbed that ass, and we started kissing all wild and shit. I was trying to get her panties off her. I wanted to smell that pussy, I wanted to taste it. I wanted to know what it felt like. I had that forbidden urge inside of me just like she did. I was a true Memphis nigga. I was 'bout that taboo shit.

"Come on then, Danyelle. Fuck it, I'll take that virginity." I gripped that ass even tighter.

She squealed and jumped off me. She stood on the side of the bed and slid her panties down her hips. The second I saw her natural pussy I felt myself turning into an animal. I scooped her ass into the air and tossed her on the bed before I got between those thighs. I kissed her neck and worked my way down to her pretty ass titties. I pulled the shirt upward, exposing them. Her nipples were like erect gumdrops. My tongue circled them, then I was sucking on them as if they were filled with milk.

She humped into me. "Fuck sucking my titties, Ja-Michael, put that dick in me. I need you to fuck me. Please, I need you so bad." She opened her thighs as wide as she could breathing heavy.

I slid down her body and planted a juicy kiss right on her pussy. The sex lips compressed against the ones on my face. I sucked them both into my mouth, then spread them apart so I could see her glistening pink. It looked so good and forbidden. Her clit poked out at the top of her hood like the tip of a pinky finger.

"Please, JaMichael, please get yo' ass up here and fuck me already." She started to shake.

I slurped her clit into my mouth and ran my tongue in circles around it. I started making all kinds of nasty noises while I went down on her. My dick was rock hard and throbbing between my legs. When I nipped her Pearl with my teeth she screamed.

"Uhhhh! Uhhhh! Uhhhhh-shit, JaMichael!" Then she started shaking as if she was having a seizure.

Bubbie started beating on the front door. I knew it was her because she'd been blowing the horn to her Range Rover the whole time I was going down on Danyelle. I wanted to ignore her ass. I wanted to fuck Danyelle so bad, but I knew there was a time and a place for everything. She lived in the same house I did, and it seemed she was addicted to that taboo shit just as much as I was. So, I knew I would get my chance to see what them walls felt like. It was just a matter of time.

***

When I opened the front door, Bubbie was standing with her hands on her hips and had a mug on her face. She looked pissed. "Nigga, I know damn well it ain't taking you this long to get ready." She looked me up and down. "Then it don't seem like you did shit."

I eased out of the house, I didn't want her to step inside because Danyelle was still lying in my bed twisted. My last sights were of her rubbing her lil young pussy, and slowly easing her middle finger inside of herself. It was amazing that I had even been able to step away from her. "I told you I was just waking up. I laid my ass back down and wound up falling back to sleep," I lied.

She smacked her lips. "Yeah, right nigga. Which one of those ratchet ass hoes do you got in your crib, right now?" She tried to push me to the side.

I held her ass. "Bubbie calm down. Ain't nobody even in here but my lil' cousin Danyelle, and she sleep," I lied again.

"Yeah, right, I ain't tryna hear that. Let me go in here and see for myself." She brushed my hands off her and nudged me aside.

At that point, I didn't give a fuck. I was irritated, and she was getting on my last nerve. On top of that, I couldn't stop thinking about how good Danyelle's lil young ass pussy looked. I wanted in. "A'ight, gone head then. Gone in there and tell me who's inside."

She stepped into the house. "I sure am." I watched her disappear into the house.

I stayed on the porch fuming. When I looked to my left, and down the street I cursed under my breath. The sun was just starting to peek through the clouds, and just as the street was becoming lit by the sun's rays, I saw Tamia rolling down the street on her bike. Even from afar I could make out her thick, well-oiled thighs. She seemed to be rocking a pair of biker shorts.

"Shit, here goes the drama."

Tamia rolled up and smiled as she got off her bike and placed it on the steps. "Hey daddy, you happy to see me?"

I came down the stairs and took a hold of her wrist. "Baby, follow me, I need to talk to you like asap."

She frowned and left her bike right where it was. "Baby, what is the matter?"

I pulled her ass into the middle of the block. I kept looking back over my shoulder to see if Bubbie had come out of the house yet. I knew there was a good chance she was going to catch Danyelle in action, and that was sure to bring about some drama. If she saw Tamia too all hell was sure to break loose. I didn't want to get Tamia all emotional and shit, and I didn't want to run Bubbie off before me and Getty could cop from her. At the same time, she was supposed to be pregnant with my child, so I needed to keep her closer than my shadow. When we were at a good spot, more than halfway down the block, I stepped in front of her. "Baby, you already know I'm trying to get Jahliya back by any means, right?"

She nodded. "Of course, I know that. Why are you pulling me all the way down here to tell me that?"

"Chill, that ain't it. Well, I gotta hit the niggas who got her with a hunnit racks a week."

"A hundred thousand dollars?" She gasped.

"Hell yeah, a hunnit bands or they gon' kill my sister."

"Okay, so why are you bringing me all the way down here?" she asked, looking over my shoulder.

"Because Bubbie's in Veronica's house, right now. I didn't want y'all to get into it."

Tamia's eyes lowered and her face turned into an evil frown. "What the fuck is she doing inside of Veronica's house, JaMichael? Have you been fucking her all night or something?" she asked, all nasty like.

"Here we go wit' this bullshit. Ain't nobody thinking about fuckin' her. I just need her so I can cop some more work and shit. On top of that, she got the plugs on all of the fiends. You can have all of the dope in the world, but it don't mean shit if you ain't got nobody to sell it to."

Tamia sucked her teeth. "JaMichael, you don't need that bitch for shit. Anything she can do I can do. All you gotta do is put a little more faith in me. Look." She adjusted the purse she was carrying on her side and dug out a wad of fifty-dollar bills and handed them to me.

"What the fuck is this?" I asked.

"It's ten of the fifteen thousand you needed." She smiled, and then musta imagined Bubbie's face because she frowned again. "You can use it to get your sister back, or at least to help pay the bill for her this week."

I flicked through the money. There was nothing there but fifties, and hundreds. "Tamia, where the fuck you get this money?"

She lowered her head and looked off. "Damn, baby, don't worry about all of that. Just know when it comes down to the get down I am willing to do whatever it takes to get you right. I'm telling you, you don't need no other bitch but me. I'm 'bout that life for you, JaMichael." She ducked down and sprinted on the side of a house that was on our street.

I looked over my shoulder and saw Bubbie come out of Veronica's house. She stood on the porch looking down the wrong side of the street for me. "Fuck."

Tamia waved me off. "Gon' head and fuck wit' her, JaMichael. Sooner or later you're going to learn where your bread is really buttered. That bitch ain't shit but a cut-throat."

Bubbie looked down the street and saw me. "Ja-Michael!" She waved me over.

I stood there for a minute and looked at Tamia from the corner of my eyes. "Baby, on my mother Blaze, rest in peace, I love you! I don't give a fuck about this bitch. I only love you. Don't let my survival fool you." I meant that shit too.

"JaMichael, just gone, I don't wanna hear that bullshit you're kicking. Tell that to the next dumb broad. I ain't the one." She crouched down on the side of the house and waved me off once again.

"Fuck what you talking about, I love you, Boo. I swear all of this shit is going to make sense in the end."

Bubbie came off the porch and started walking up to me. I looked back once, and made eye contact with Tamia, she was looking evil as hell. She moved further on to the side of the house until she was no longer visible.

Bubbie came to me and wrapped her arms around my neck. "Baby, I'm sorry for doubting you. I see you really were telling the truth. There was nobody in the house but your little cousin, and baby you won't believe what I caught her little ass doing in your bed?" She snickered and leaned further into me.

"What's that?" I asked.

"Well, let's just say her and I got real acquainted. It turns out that your lil' cousin is a boss freak. I like her lil' ass."

"Is that so?" I put my arm around her shoulder so I could walk her back in the other direction.

"I mean you should know, after all, she was playing with her pussy on your bed. It looks to me like y'all was in there on some real Memphis type shit," she said, looking up at me. "Is that true?"

I held my silence, I didn't know how to answer her question. I also didn't feel like answering it or explaining myself anyway. I waited until we were in her Range Rover, and she was pulling away from the curb before I responded.

"If we was on that what you gon' do about it?" I waited until she turned her head before I grabbed the Crown Royal knapsack she had on the passenger seat. I tucked the money Tamia had just given me inside of it and placed the bag under the seat in two-fluid motions.

She giggled and kept her focus on getting into the busy intersection. "Shit, she fine as hell, I wouldn't blame you. She got them pretty ass light brown eyes, and her body all sexy and shit. I don't even fuck wit hoes, but I'd get down with you and her in a heartbeat. Besides, y'all ain't the only family that got secrets. This is Memphis, tell me who ain't got skeletons in their closet?" She reached over and located my dick, squeezing it. "So, are you fuckin' Danyelle?"

I let her fondle me for a seconds before I pushed her hand away. "That ain't none of yo' bidness. You stay in yo' own lane and I'll stay in mine. Now, what's the real reason you're hitting me up so early in the morning?"

She removed her hand from my lap. "You'll see when you get to my father's mansion. Until then, it's cool with me if we just ride, and listen to music. I don't even wanna talk to yo' ass, right now." She clicked something on her phone, and a song by *Jill Scott* came crooning out of the radio.

I sat back and got comfortable if she didn't wanna talk to me, I didn't wanna talk to her ass either.

Ghost

Chapter 8

Bubbie's crib was decked out in candles when I got inside of it. It smelled like Prada incense, and she had her fireplace roaring. She took off her red-bottomed heels, set them on the side of the door and instructed me to take off my shoes as well. Since I was accustomed to doing exactly that when it came to Veronica's crib I wasn't tripping. She took hold of my hand after I was shoeless and led me into the massive living room. Directly in the center of it was a huge Brunch platter set up. She even had the clear pitchers of orange juice chilling on ice.

"You see, JaMichael, I just wanted to spend some quality time with, my baby daddy. Screw all the hustling, and bustling for a day, and kick back with the mother of your child." She kissed me on the cheek and rubbed my chest for a second. "Come on let's eat, baby."

A female maid stepped out of the shadows and nearly caused me to jump out of my skin. It wasn't until the candlelight illuminated her uniform, and I saw her face, that I understood who she was, and what was going on. "Senor, and Señora, how can I accommodate you?" She asked in broken English.

Bubbie looked up at me and smiled once again. "Baby do you think we need a butler slash maid? Or can we handle all this stuff on our own?" She batted her eyelashes.

I looked over the maid, she looked to be about forty years old, athletic, with a gorgeous face. At least she looked as good as the candlelight would allow her too. "I don't know, baby. I ain't never been served before. I think that might be cool." I peeped how short the skirt on the maid was.

She had a nice pair of thighs. Her perfume even smelled good. I didn't know what my problem was but when it came to women I could barely control myself. I think I needed to see a therapist.

"Rosa, you can start by popping that champagne for us. Then you can hook us up with a nice Brunch platter," Bubbie ordered, wrapping her arms around my neck.

I held her small waists and kissed her lips, even though, I wasn't really feeling being on that lovey-dovey shit with her. I still had Tamia heavy on my mind, along with Jahliya's situation. "Baby, you, already know you ain't have to put together all of this just so I could spend some time with you. I had planned on doing that anyway."

She grunted. "I couldn't tell, JaMichael, you're the only nigga I know that could go weeks at a time without talking to me. Do you have any idea how that makes me feel?" she asked, guiding my hand so that I sat beside her on the pallet that was made for our romantic brunch.

"You already know how these streets are, and you know what I'm up against when it comes to getting my sister back. I ain't got time to be wasting any precious seconds. I gotta be in those streets until I meet the quota that Mikey's bitch ass placed on me every single week. You ain't got the slightest idea what I'm going through, right now." I leaned all the way back until I was resting on my elbows.

She laid beside me and rubbed my stomach. "Baby, I don't know exactly what you're going through. I won't until you explain to me what's really going on. You're my baby daddy now. Were supposed to be in this it together. It's supposed to be us against the world."

I grabbed her hand, threw it off my stomach, got up and walked over and turned on the lights. I was heated. She made her way to her feet and gave me a look that told me she was confused. I waved off the maid. "Shawty give us a few minutes."

She bowed her head and left out of the room. On her way out I still couldn't help glancing down at her ass. It jiggled through her tight skirt and continued to rise with every step she took.

"Baby, what's the matter?" Bubbie asked, stepping in front of me, trying to rest her hands on my chest.

Once again, I removed them with one hand and with the other one I grabbed her by the throat and forced her back into the wall, while she beat at my hands. Once her back was planted against the wall, I lifted her up with one hand and had her feet dangling off of the ground.

"Ack! Ack! Ack!" she choked.

"Bitch, how the fuck you gon' act like you're riding with me when your, muthafuckin' cousin is a part of the Duffle Bag Cartel. That nigga probably knows where my sister at, right now. And you're sitting around this ma'fucka acting like everything is cool. I should stank yo' simple ass," I said, choking her harder and harder.

Now she was really beating at my hands. Her eyes were bugging out of her head. Tears sailed down her cheeks. I lifted her higher, then dropped her to the carpet. She fell to her knees coughing and hacking her lungs. I didn't give no fuck.

"Damn you, JaMichael. How the fuck you gon' treat yo' baby mama like that?" she groaned, before coughing all over again.

"Bitch, how the fuck you gon act like yo' cousin ain't plugged with them niggas that's got my sister missing in action? This is a two-way street. I know you got my shorty, and all that shit, but it still only holds so much weight."

She crawled across the floor crying now. "Ghost, I ain't have nothing to do with that. That's between y'all. All I care about is you, and this baby growing inside me. I hope you don't think you finna be putting yo' hands on me all the time either?" she said rising to her feet. Her eyes were still bloodshot.

"Like I said, bitch, I ain't trying to hear none of that. Every time I look at you, I see that nigga Mikey, and that fuck nigga Phoenix. Phoenix got your blood, so in my eyes, you muthafuckas are equivalent to each other."

She shook her head. "Jam, I would never choose Phoenix over you. I been loving you since way before we ever started messing around. All you gotta do is tell me what you need from me. Anything you need from me, I'll do it. I'm that crazy about you."

"Bitch that nigga talking about he wants a hunnit gees a week. How much are you going to help me come up with weekly?"

She ran her fingers through her hair. "A hundred thousand? Ghost, that's a whole lot of money." She started biting her manicured fingernails.

"Exactly, that's what I thought. So, when you're trying to hit up my phone and I ain't picking it up you should know that I'm in the streets trying to make shit happen since ain't nobody else trying to help me. You can't holla that love shit if you aren't willing to do what it takes to love me unconditionally. Tamia willing to do anythang for me. I got a few gees in your truck, right now that she came up on to help me get my sister back. She ain't even in the streets, but she playing in these ma'fuckas to make sure I'm able to meet that quota. That's a real bitch, right there."

Bubbie smacked her lips. "I ain't trying to hear nothing you're expressing about her. You and her just got a thing for each other. That's the only reason you're giving her so many props." She rolled her eyes. "Come upstairs, I got something for you."

I shook my head. "Fuck sex, if that's all you have to offer me, you can keep that shit to yourself. I mean that."

"JaMichael, would you bring your ass upstairs? Damn, why you acting like an ass hole and shit?"

I needed to throw Tamia in her face some more. I knew that the key to getting Bubbie to step her game all the way up was that I had to get her into competition with Tamia. They hated each other. That was no secret. If I could somehow find a way to get both females bringing me their A-game, along with me giving my all. Instead of me having to wait damn near ten weeks before I got Jahliya back, I could get her from under the Duffle Bag Cartel in half the time.

"Bubbie, what you got for me upstairs?"

She exhaled loud enough for me to hear her. I could tell she was getting irritated, and I didn't give no fuck. "Ja-Michael, all you gotta do is come up here, and find out. Nigga, how hard is that?"

The next thing I knew we were heading upstairs, and she was directing me into her bedroom. She wanted me to sit on the bed, but instead, I continued to stand by her white dresser. Before she left out the room, Tamia hit me up.

Tamia: *JaMichael, you bet not be fuckin' with Bubbie ass. You need to bring yo ass to see me asap!*

Bubbie saw me reading the text and placed her hand on her hip. "Who the fuck is that, JaMichael?"

"Tamia," I said being honest. "She's worried about me and told me to get at her as soon as possible." I texted Tamia back.

JaMichael: *Nah, babe…I ain't fuckin' wit' Bubbie. I'll be back your way in about a half-hour or so. Don't trip!*

I put my phone in my pocket.

Bubbie rolled her eyes. "Just stay right here, JaMichael. I'll be right back."

The entire time she was gone I kept seeing Jahliya's face inside my mind. I decided right then that before I gave Mikey the first payments of his cash, I had to see my sister. I was missing her like crazy and needed to see her, it was as simple as that. Bubbie appeared five minutes later with a small knapsack. Instead of her handing the sack to me she tossed it on the bed. A few knots of cash fell out.

"That's fifty thousand dollars in cash, right there, Ja-Michael. Now I know you can come up with the remainder of what you need before your deadline. You're a street nigga, but this should at least prevent you from having to be in the streets for as long as you originally planned. I am willing to do my part for you, JaMichael as long as it's us, and not no other bitch, and you know what I mean."

I was already going through the money. It was five bands of ten thousand. The bills looked like they'd been around. I could already tell this was trap money. "Bubbie, you think I'm one of them low class, take the bottom of the barrel type niggas or something? Shawty you actually think you doing something by hitting me with this chump change? Don't you know I'll burn this shit, then go out there and make shit happen for Jahliya anyway?"

"But you ain't gotta do all that. I'm willing to meet you halfway as long as you're in this mess. As long as I know we are together. All I'm asking is that you make shit official between you and me. In fact, if you do I ain't got no problem coming up with seventy-five thousand a week, every week. That's how much I care about you."

"Bitch, if you cared about me you would come up with that type of cash anyway. Love is supposed to be unconditional. Right now, what you're doing is stating the condition, and terms it's going to take for you to love me."

"JaMichael, you know damn well I didn't mean it like that. All I'm asking is for you to claim me before my pregnancy belly starts showing. Is that too much to ask?" She stepped into my face and looked into my eyes with her pretty ones.

I started thinking about her coming up with seventy-five bands every single week. I imagined how easy that would make my job. All I wanted was to get my sister home safe and sound. Every night that she was away from me felt as if I had a dagger placed in my heart. Bubbie had just handed me fifty gees as if it was the most natural thing in the world, and even though I was making light of the situation it really was a big deal. I didn't know a lot of niggas that had a female who would drop them off fifty thousand dollars in cash as if it were light work. So, I had to keep Bubbie as close as a shadow.

"So, what are you thinking, JaMichael? Do you think I'm asking too much of you?" she asked, popping back on her legs, looking me over.

"If I let you do that are you about to go and get another twenty-five bands, right now? Is that what you're telling me?"

She smiled. "That's exactly what I'm saying. I know what you're trying to do, JaMichael. Even though Phoenix, is my cousin *by marriage*, let's not forget that. I don't have nothing to do with what he and Mikey are doing. That's not my business. They won't listen to me, but I can help you with this financially. What do you say?"

All I could do was take a deep breath and nod my head. "A'ight, do what you need to do. After you give me that cash, though."

She squealed and wrapped her arms around my neck.

Chapter 9

Tamia held her computer on her lap and cried her eyes out. "Are you fuckin kidding me, JaMichael? Really, you gon' let this bitch announce to the world that y'all are a couple and that she's having your baby? What the fuck is going on?"

I stood before her sick with it, Bubbie had gone hard all over social media. She made sure everybody she could reach knew she and I were together, even though, I wasn't seeing shit that way. In my heart, I felt I was doing whatever it took to get the finances in order to ensure, that I would have Jahliya's fee every week. Mikey had already shut down my request to see Jahliya. I was set to drop off the first hundred thousand dollars this night.

Tamia jumped up and dropped the laptop on the floor. "Answer me, JaMichael?" Tears ran down her face. "What are you doing with this bitch behind my back? Why is she claiming you on social media now and promoting that she's giving birth to your child?"

"Tamia, I don't feel like doing this shit, baby. Please let's not get into this. I gotta go and meet Mikey in less than an hour. I gotta have my head on straight, you know that."

"Nigga that's an hour from now. I need to know what the fuck is going on, right now. I love you way too much to let you do me like you're doing. I swear to God, Ja-Michael." She balled her little fists and stepped into my face with her nostrils flaring.

I took a step back and stretched my arms out. "Tamia, you, already know I ain't with you getting in my face. Back yo' ass up and we can talk about this like adults."

She pushed my arms downward and found a way to step right back in my grill. "Tell me what the fuck is going on or so help me God!" she snapped as tears ran down her face so much now that she had to keep blinking her eyes. The water dripped off her chin and ran down her neck.

"Baby, I need this bitch."

"You need her?" She squeezed her eyelids together. "I thought you needed me. I been out there doing everything I can to help you come up with this money. Things I would have never even thought about doing. But I've been doing them because you mean the world to me, and I would do anything for you. You are my whole life, JaMichael. So, explain to me why you need this bitch over me? What does she have on me?"

"Tamia, I never said I needed her over you. I ain't never said that she had shit on you."

"You don't have to, JaMichael! You're saying that shit by letting this bitch claim you on Facebook. She telling everybody y'all are a couple, and that y'all are going to be this one big happy family. She calling you, Daddy and Bae. Fuck, JaMichael, I thought you were my Daddy? That you were my Bae?" She fell to her knees and hollered into her hands. I could see her tears running down her wrists as she rocked back and forth. "I just don't understand. I try so hard for you. I do everything I can for you and it's never enough," she cried some more. "Why the fuck do I even try?" she questioned.

She made a lump form in my throat. I slowly kneeled beside her and tried to wrap her arm around her neck. But she jumped up and backed all the way into the wall as if she were repulsed at my attempt to console her. This made me feel sick on my stomach because I really loved and cared about Tamia. If I ever imagined myself marrying anybody way down in the distant future, I saw myself marrying her, and being with her faithfully. But that shit would have to be all the way down the line. I was nowhere near that point yet, that was for sure.

"Baby, what the fuck?"

She wiped her tears away. "You're killing me, Ja-Michael. Can't you see how much weight I'm losing? Can't you tell by my hair? My shit been in a ponytail for damn near a month. I ain't had my nails done. I been rocking the same two fits and you ain't even noticed. That's what's so fuckin' sad. It's sad because you don't care about me. You don't care about nobody other than yourself."

I stood up, closed the door and locked it. I looked across the room at her. "You really believe that shit, huh?"

She nodded. "I really do. You didn't stop for one second to even consider how this whole thing was going to make me feel. On top of that, you didn't even act like you wanted to check this broad for claiming that y'all are a couple. That's how I know there is more at play. I know you got something going on with her that you're trying to hide from me. That's what's killing me, right now because it isn't fair." She slowly slid down the wall and wound up with her knees to her chest. She wrapped her arms around them. "I never thought you would hurt me like this, Ja-Michael. I never thought you would ever hurt your, baby girl. You got me so fragile." She covered her face with her hands and cried into them again.

I shook my head and swallowed, I hated to hear her cry. For me, it was the worst sound in the world. I sat beside her and pulled her to me. She seemed to try and break away, but I held her. She was no match for my strength.

"Tamia, listen, baby. I'm sorry! That shit she's posting ain't real. That bitch asked me to do that. She said it was the only way she would help me with the money that I need to get Jahliya back. You should already know I don't love nobody as much as I love you. I mean other than my sister. I'm just playing my role, right now to get what I need out of her ass." I rested my lips against the side of her forehead.

She allowed me to hold her for a moment, then she pushed me off her and stood back up. "Do you have any idea how bogus you sound, right now, JaMichael?"

I stood up irritated. I didn't want to go on and on about the same ass thing. "Fuck is yo' problem now? I'm trying my best to ask for forgiveness. You making this shit real hard."

"Nigga, is that what you call yourself doing? All I hear is that you're constantly calling the girl that is about to have your child a bitch. That's first off. Secondly, you're telling me that you're basically using your baby mother to be just so you can get Jahliya back. While I would understand that if she was a regular-ass broad, but she's not, she's the mother of your child to be. That's foul. Lastly, you're trying to convince me that you're in the right in all of this garbage, when clearly you are playing both sides. That's so bogus of you, JaMichael. You're acting tricky as hell."

By this time, I was so irritated I didn't care to reason with her anymore. Besides, it was hard to argue with a female especially when they were all the way in the right. So, instead of trying to use mental manipulation to get what I wanted I decided to just keep shit all the way real. "You know what Tamia, baby I love you, but you can't produce what old girl can. If you could I wouldn't need her, but you can't so I do. It's as simple as that."

She mugged me and balled her fist tight. Tears eased out of her eye again. "JaMichael, I'm sorry I ain't financially got what that bitch do." She sniffed snot back into her nose. I could tell she was really messed up on the inside. "I'm sorry all I can offer you at this age is my unconditional love. I wish I could go out and get you all the money you need, but I can't. I can only stand beside you and do the best I can even when you treat me like shit. That has to count for something." She lowered her head and took a deep breath, before sitting on the edge of the bed.

"It do, and I wish it counted toward the shit Mikey and his crew are asking to receive in exchange for, Jahliya, but it don't. So, I gotta do what I gotta do."

"And that means you gotta be in this couple with Bubbie, right? That means y'all gotta parade around on social media as if y'all are this one big happy family in the making? That means I gotta see this bitch repping my nigga, even though, I already know she ain't willing to die for you the way that I am. I'll die for you, right now, JaMichael, and you know I will, don't you?"

"Baby I—"

"Nigga, are you strapped?"

"What?"

"You heard me, JaMichael. I asked you are you strapped?" She wiped her tears away and swallowed her spit.

"Yeah, you already know I don't leave home without it."

She waved me off. "I ain't trying to hear all that tough guy shit. Ghost, pull out that ma'fucka. I wanna see it, right now."

"See what?" I asked, playing dumb. I didn't know what she was up too, but it was making me severely uncomfortable.

"Pull out your gun, JaMichael. Let me see it, now boy!"

I grabbed the pistol from the small of my back and turned away from her. I pulled out the clip, and took the one out of the chamber, before turning back around to her.

"See, this how it looks. Are you happy?" I slipped the contents of the gun into my back pocket. It appeared she was too busy fixated on the sight of the gun to notice.

She ignored me and held her hand out. "Give it to me."

"What?"

"JaMichael, stop playin' wit' me, and let me see that fuckin' gun." When I neglected to move, she sighed and shook her hand in front of me. "Gimme the fuckin' gun. I bet if Bubbie asked you to see your gun you would break your neck to give it to her."

I pulled her close and placed the gun on her chest. "Here, take this ma'fucka. Fuck is you gon' do wit' it, though?"

She turned it to the side and flipped it off safety. Then she took five steps back. "I told you I would die for you, right, JaMichael?"

"Yeah, you said that and what?"

She sniffed hard and brought the snot back into her nose that had been on her upper lip. "JaMichael, I can't have you being with no other female if it ain't me. You were designed for me, and I for you. I feel that deep within the pits of my soul. I'd rather die if I can't have you all to myself, I swear to God." She cocked the hammer and placed the gun to her temple.

My eyes got bucked. "Tamia, what the fuck are you doing?"

She blinked more tears from her eyes. "JaMichael, it has to be me and you. If it's not then ain't no reason for me to be here."

"Tamia, you acting real weak, right now. Gimme that fuckin' gun," I snapped taking a step toward her.

She stepped back and shook her head. "Don't come any closer, JaMichael. Just tell me you love me. Tell me you love me more than, Bubbie. Say it!"

"Tamia, I don't love that bitch at all. You're the female outside of my sister that I do love. Now give me that fuckin' gun and quit acting so weak. You supposed to be a soldier."

"Tell me you're done fuckin' wit', Bubbie."

"Tamia, stop acting stupid. Gimme the fuckin' gun. Now!"

"I'm not a soldier, JaMichael. I love you too much to be a soldier. I'm weak and since I know you ain't done fuckin' wit' her, I'd rather just let y'all be happy. You don't love me fa real anyway." She took a deep breath and pulled the trigger three quick times. The gun clicked each time. She pulled it from her temple, pointed it toward her face and pulled it over and over again.

I smacked the gun from her hand. It dropped to the floor with a loud thump and slid under the bed. Then I snatched her by the blouse and brought her to me. "Bitch you was finna sit here, and kill yo' muthafuckin' self, over this emotional ass shit?"

"I'm tired, JaMichael. I'm so tired, and you're killing me anyway. Every time you go to her you're killing me. I can't take it no more. Why didn't that gun work? Please fix it, I don't wanna be here no more," she cried, dropping to her knees, crawling across the floor, and grabbing the pistol from under the bed. She sat cross-legged looking it over. "Fix it for me, Daddy. I can't take this shit no longer, it hurts too bad." Snot ran down her lip. She peered up at me with red eyes, pleading for mercy.

It made me feel weak, I kneeled beside her and took the gun away. "Baby, please, just listen to me." I kneeled so that I was facing her, grabbed her shoulders and shook her. "I don't give a fuck about that bitch. All I care about is the money. I love you, I have always loved you, Tamia. Damn, why can't you get that through your head?"

She continued to cry, she looked so vulnerable. I hated seeing her in that state. I knew she loved me more than Bubbie ever really could. I also knew I was hurting her, but my immaturity didn't allow me to have the remedy to fix the problem. I needed both her and Bubbie for two different reasons. It was about more than love for me, it was about survival. Love wouldn't bring Jahliya home from her captors, only money would.

Tamia wiped away her tears. "Just kill me, JaMichael, please. I am begging you to kill me." She scooted away from me and kneeled on the floor with her face in the carpet. "I can't take this, JaMichael. I need you to send me on my way."

All I could do was pull her back into my arms and hold her until she cried herself to sleep. I told her over and over how much I loved her. It took a whole lot of convincing, but before it was all said and done we came to a brief understanding. I was to make Bubbie take down the statuses online, and the dealings I had with Bubbie was supposed to become less and less. She fell asleep in my arms as soon as our agreement came into place. I didn't know how I was going to amend shit with Bubbie, but I would have too because I cared about Tamia's feelings.

Chapter 10

Later that night, me and Getty met Mikey, and five niggas from his Duffle Bag Cartel Crew under the train station's viaduct. When we pulled into the meeting spot the first thing I noticed was that all the lights that had previously been used to illuminate things had been busted out. When we pulled up to them, Mikey was standing in front of a Jaguar truck's headlights. He held a .40 Glock in each hand, and a red rag over his face. His goons looked to be spread out strategically. They were armed with assault rifles.

I was the first to step out of Getty's Ford Expedition. I had two .40 calibers in my waistband, and the duffle bag filled with the hundred thousand dollars. The air felt hot and moist. There were bugs flying all over the place. They were crashing into my face and all type of shit. But I didn't allow myself to focus on that. I wanted to get Mikey his money and go from there.

I stepped to Mikey's Jaguar truck and slammed the bag on top of it. "Here you go right here, homie. This a hunnit gees in cash. The first payment, I'll be back real soon with the second."

Mikey didn't say a word. He brushed past me and un-zipped the bag. His men cocked their weapons and got ready to blow both me and Getty away I assumed. "Nigga, you betta hope all of the money is here. If you're missing one red cent that's a strike. You gon' have one more of them before I'm forced to handle my bidness with Jahliya the nasty way, and then directly afterward you're more than likely to find her lil' ass floating in a creek, half-eaten by Alligators." This made him snicker like a true bitch nigga. "This shit is serious." He began rifling through the bag.

"Yousa a clown. What the fuck I look like shortchanging you when you got my sister's life in your hands?" I was imagining everything he'd just said, and the image pissed me off so bad I began to sweat all down my back.

Mikey pulled up a couple of stacks and looked them over. Tossed them back inside of the bag, zipped it and tossed it to one of his lil' homies. "Put that shit into my truck, Mane and hurry the fuck up." His goon followed the orders immediately. "Say, JaMichael, I got some bidness I need you to take care of."

I stepped closer to him and frowned. I was already wondering what this fool had up his sleeve. I knew he was one of the dirtiest niggas in Memphis. I hated him wit' a passion and already knew before it was all said and done, I was going to get him for what he was doing to Jahliya. "Fuck bidness you think you got for me, Homeboy?"

He laughed. "Nigga, for a muthafucka that got his back against the wall, you show be acting like you're tough as a bitch. What would you do if I told you, I already knocked your sister's head clean off her shoulders?" he asked, with a sadistic smirk.

I imagined him hurting her for the hundredth time that night. The visual was enough to make me choke up in anger. It was taking all the willpower I had inside of me to not pull out my guns and start bussing. I wanted to see what Mikey's brains would look like on the outside of his face. I wanted to torture his ass. I wanted to skin him alive. I still couldn't believe how much I'd failed Jahliya.

"Nigga, on my mother in heaven, if I ever find out you hurt my sister in any way I'm bodying every nigga and bitch you're close top. I want yo' head already. Now tell me that Jahliya is anything other than alive, we gon' kick this war off, right now. Ain't no sense in waitin'."

He stood in my face, clenching his jaw as if he didn't know what to say or do. I could tell he was heated. The headlights from his Jaguar truck was the only lights that we were working off. But it was all of the light that I needed in order to see his emotions that were written all over his mug. "Nigga, you must be talking all that shit because you think I'ma have mercy on you because you're parading around with Phoenix's lil' cousin, huh?"

"Nigga fuck you, I don't know who you're talking about," I said, ready to slide my hand under my shirt and put his ass to sleep indefinitely.

"Bubbie, nigga, she might be the only reason I'ma give you a chance to straighten up your act before I slump you. You already know I don't like you, JaMichael."

"Nigga I don't like yo' bitch ass either, you ain't said shit but a word." I stepped in his face.

He took a step back and pushed me so hard I flew into his truck and put a dent in it. It also knocked the wind out of me. I fell to my knees, trying to catch my breath. "You, pussy ass nigga," I wheezed.

Getty rushed to my side with his pistol out. "JaMichael, you okay?" he asked, worried.

I pushed him off me and struggled to get up. I felt like he'd just gotten off on me. I had to keep Jahliya at the forefront of my brain, or I was set to make a horrible decision that could cost my sister her life.

"Nigga I'm tired of you always acting like you so muthafuckin' hard. Yousa Peon, I'll twist yo' muthafuckin' cap nigga, with no hesitation," he threatened.

Getty jumped up, as soon as he did Mikey upped both of his. 40 Glocks under his chin and cocked the hammers. "Move fuck nigga. Act like you 'bout that life, and I'ma show you, you ain't on shit. Gimme this muthafucka!" He snatched his Tech right from his hand and tossed it to one of his lil' Hittas.

Getty held his hands up. "A'ight nigga, you got me. I ain't on shit."

"Nigga I know you ain't." Mikey kissed him on the cheek. "Yo' lil' bitch ass is as sweet as bear meat. Lay on the ground," he ordered.

Getty hesitated. "What?"

"You heard me, and I swear on my crew if I gotta say it again you gon feel at least a hunnit slugs. Get-yo-bitch-ass-on-the-ground, now, nigga!"

Getty musta thought about it for a second because he froze. Then he kept his hands raised and slowly lowered himself to the ground. "A'ight nigga, I'm doing everything you said."

Mikey's men closed in around him. All of them were heavily armed and ready to blow something back. Once again, I was ready to pull out my strap. If Jahliya didn't continuously cross my mind I would have. The Duffle Bag Cartel had us right where they wanted us. If they even attempted to blow us back, they could have and probably would have gotten away with it. There was a creek full of alligators not more than five miles away. I was familiar with bodies being chopped up, and thrown inside of that creek, most of the street niggas in Memphis was.

Mikey stepped over to Getty's body and kicked him as hard as he could in the ribs. Getty curled into a ball. Mikey raised his foot and brought it down hard directly into Getty's ribs. Getty hollered out and jumped up. Before he could get far, Mikey aimed and fired his gun three times.

Boom! Boom! Boom!

"Noooo!" I yelled.

84

Getty fell to his knees as soon as the slugs entered into his back. He fell face-first on the concrete and started to exhale back to back with blood leaking out of his body. "Uhhhh. Uhhhh. Uhhhh," he groaned.

I rushed to his side and kneeled beside him. I pulled him into my arms. Tears were already coming out of my eyes. "Getty! Getty! Get up man, get yo' ass up," I hollered, ready to lose my mind.

"Nigga that's for when you smoked my lil' nigga the other day. What you thought it was sweet or something?" Mikey asked, with a big smile on his face.

I continued to situate Getty in my arms. He was bleeding profusely. "Getty fight, bruh. Nigga, I need you. You already know we gon' get these niggas back. All you gotta do is fight. Fight for your brother man."

Mikey came and stood over him. He hawked and spit a big yellow loogey in Getty's face. "Bitch nigga, I hope you die." He snickered. "Cartel, we out." He walked to his Jaguar and opened the door. "JaMichael, this shit ain't over. You owe me a favor on top of my hunnit a week. I been handling you with baby hands. You wanna act like a Killa, nigga I'ma treat you like one. I hope ya boy die." He got into his truck and pulled out of the parking lot with his savages in tow.

Getty started to shake in my arms. By this time the concrete was covered in his blood. I held him tight and called the paramedics with my cellphone. After they assured me they were on their way, I hung up and continued to hold my nigga. I had so much hatred beaming through me, I could barely think straight. I was also praying that Getty didn't die.

***

I disappeared when I heard the sirens pulling into the railroad station. I couldn't allow Twelve to catch me kneeling over Getty's body. I knew they would have too many questions. Questions I couldn't answer. So, I stayed at a close distance and waited until they snatched him up. I followed close behind, and when I saw them pull into Saint Mary's hospital, I went around the long way and parked my car. I broke down behind the wheel. Tears just started coming out of my eyes rapidly. I couldn't believe how Mikey was fucking me over. First, he'd taken my sister, now he'd shot up my right-hand man. Spit all in his face and treated me like a bitch. I didn't know how much more I could take without completely losing my mind.

***

I got to Tamia's house at three o'clock that morning. I simply climbed into her bedroom window and slid into the bed with her before she even knew I was there. When she opened her eyes and saw it was me she jerked her head back and looked concerned. "Baby what's the matter? What happened?"

I blinked tears again, I wasn't the crying type, but I was hurting worse than ever. I felt I had dropped the ball twice, first with Jahliya, and now with Getty. "Baby, I don't wanna talk about it tonight. I'll tell you in the morning. For now, I just wanna hold you, and go to sleep. I need you. Just you, Tamia, please tell me I can have you."

She nodded. "Every day and for the rest of my life. Come on, Daddy, we'll face whatever you're going through together, in the morning. I got you, and I love you."

"I love you, too, boo! Now let's go to sleep." I held her so tight she winced in pain. She gathered herself, then she was rubbing my forearms until we drifted off.

Ghost

Chapter 11

Bubbie found out what happened to Getty and took it upon herself to drop two hundred thousand dollars for Mikey's fees. I didn't know where she got so much cash, and I didn't ask her. I was happy to get Mikey off of my case for two weeks so I could regroup. To be honest, Mikey had fucked my mind all the way up. He had me afraid to look at my own reflection in this mirror. I felt soft. I felt weak. I felt like a life sucka. I still couldn't believe I'd allowed Jahliya, and Getty to come under the gun the way that I had. All the things that took place weren't supposed to have happened if I had been on my game.

Twelve days after Getty had been admitted into the hospital for the attack Mikey had waged upon him, both me and Tamia found ourselves in St. Mary's intensive care waiting room. When we first got there Candy was already present.

When she saw me, she jumped up and rushed into my arms. "JaMichael, JaMichael! Oh my, God. Thank you for coming. He still hasn't woken up. I'm so worried, I don't know what to do. I can't raise his daughter on my own," she cried, resting her face in my shoulder.

I patted her back. "Calm down, Getty is a fighter. He ain't gon' let no lil' bullets take him out. And as far as little Angel goes, as long as I got air in my lungs, she ain't gon' have to worry about nothin'. Matter fact, I got all of your bills indefinitely."

She hugged my neck and broke down crying. "Oh my, God, JaMichael. I love you so-so much. Thank you, Lord knows you don't have to do none of the things that you're doing." She held me for a moment, then kissed my cheek.

Tamia grunted, came over and pulled her off me. "Uh, I understand you're going through some shit, but don't be putting your fuckin' lips on my man. Save that shit for, Getty." She turned to me and wiped the kiss away.

Candy frowned and looked Tamia over. She was a few inches taller than Tamia, and at least ten pounds heavier. She musta sized her up pretty quick, because the next thing I knew Candy was taking her hoop earrings out of her ears.

"Bitch, I don't give a fuck what, JaMichael is to you. If you put your filthy hands on me again, I swear to God on my baby I'ma mop the floor wit' yo' ass."

Tamia smacked her lips. "Bitch you ain't said shit! What you wanna do?" She kicked off her Jordan's and threw up her guards.

"Bitch what?" Candy, kicked off her heels and got into a fighting stance. "I'm from North Memphis, we 'bout dat dare lil' momma, let's tear this bitch up then."

I stepped in the middle of them and faced Tamia, turning my back to Candy. I rested my forehead against hers. "Baby, this moment ain't about neither one of y'all. We're supposed to be here to support, Getty. Now go over there and sit yo ass down before I spank that ass. Do you want me to do that?"

"No," she mumbled. "But Daddy this bitch acting like it's sweet just because she's a lil' bigger than me. I ain't scared of nobody but God."

"I know, Boo, and you ain't got shit to prove. Go sit down and let me handle this." I patted her on the ass. "Gon' now."

She scooted along, then stopped and picked up her Jordan's. Her thick ass cheeks jiggled in her tight jeans. She looked so good, it felt like she was starting to grow on me more and more every single day. She took a seat on the couch and crossed her thick thighs all angrily like. To me it just made her look that much finer. Especially when she crossed her arms and looked off obviously irritated.

Candy slowly slipped back into her heels. I took a hold of her arm and pulled her into the hallway right by the bathrooms. As soon as we were there, she tried to hug me, I stopped her.

"Check this out, Candy, I know you're feeling me and all that shit, but first off, you gotta have more respect for my homie than that. Secondly, that's my main bitch out there. Shawty ride or die and she fuckin' wit' me the long way. If you gon' be on that level wit' me you gon' have to respect her. That's just how this shit finna go."

"JaMichael, I ain't got no problem respecting her. She just ain't have no right putting her hands on me. I don't know that bitch from, Adam," she snapped.

"You're right, but what's done is done. Y'all had a misunderstanding. That shit's squashed, now from here on out it's gon have to be mutual respect. You understand me?"

She nodded. "JaMichael, I'll do whatever you say. You should already know how I feel about you. Getty told me, he told you and I ain't even fucked up about it because it's true. I been feeling you, and always will."

"Well, right now that shit's dead. My main focus is on my nigga and making sure his daughter is well taken care of. Anythang you feeling is gon' have to go on hold. You feel me?"

"I wish I could." She stepped into my personal space and giggled.

I ain't see shit funny. She picked up on that and smiled weakly. "Candy, I love my nigga. My brain is fucked up, right now. I need you to take his situation a little more serious."

She shook her head. "Look, JaMichael, I understand he's your boy and all, but to me, he wasn't nothing but a dead beat. He not only refused to take care of our daughter, but he used to whoop my ass like it was nobody's business. So, I'm sorry if I can't go there emotionally with you. Or if I can't continue to put up a facade in front of these white folks. I mean I hope he gets off that table, and all of that, but that would be just for Angel's sake, not mine. However, I'll do whatever you want me to do, but just know I'm doing it for the sake of my little girl, and for the sake of the love I have for you."

"If that's the motivation you have to use then do that. Like I said before, I got your bills. All I ask is that you respect my woman and allow me to be a part of Angel's life if Getty gets worse."

"I'll do both with no hesitation. In fact—" She walked past me, back into the lobby.

I followed her before she could walk up on Tamia. Tamia stood up and got ready for war. I could see she had her little fists balled up.

Candy stopped mid-stride and held her hands up. "Hey, I come in peace. I just wanted to apologize and let you know from here on out you will get nothin' but the utmost respect from me." She extended her hand.

Tamia looked it over for a few moments and shook her head. "Bitch we ain't gotta shake hands. I don't know you, but I already don't like you. I can see the way you look at my Daddy. I don't like it, you got some shit up your sleeve. You got an agenda, I can see it."

Candy snapped her head in my direction. "Damn, JaMichael, she's making this shit so hard. How the fuck am I supposed to respect her if she ain't willing to give it back in return?"

Before I could answer, the doctor, a short, white, bald-head man, with blue eyes, came over and motioned for Candy to come to him. She followed him out into the hallway where he began to talk and use his hands at the same time. He looked so animated. I was trying my best to read the expressions on her face I was having a hard time reading her though. Tamia came up beside me and rested her hand on my shoulder. "Baby, I hope she ain't getting no bad news, and it's not for her sake, but for Getty's. I know if anything happens to him you'll lose your mind. I can't have my man losing his mind like that, I need you."

Candy covered her mouth and shook her head. The doctor kept on talking. She blinked tears and wiped them away. He looked over his clipboard, and rested his hand on her arm, before walking away. Candy remained in place.

I was so anxious to find out what was going on, I made my way over to her, just as she was holding her weight up against the wall. "Man, what happened? What the doctor say?"

She covered her face with one hand as best as she could, before taking it away and wiping away her tears. "They said Getty has to undergo at least three more surgeries. Two of the bullets are still lodged in his spine. They were able to remove one, but the risk of removing another one that was only centimeters away was just too risky. So, they are going to go back in there at two o'clock this afternoon. He says they can already tell there is a ninety-five percent chance Getty will be paralyzed from the waist down.

"The reason for the additional surgeries is to try and prevent him from being paralyzed from the neck down. He's been in and out of consciousness since the event. Oh, JaMichael, all this stuff is starting to get to me. I don't know what to do, I mean me and him weren't on the best terms. But I still don't want to see nothing bad happening to him, it's not fair." She came over and wrapped her arms around me.

I held her for a second before I peered into Tamia's eyes. She frowned and looked off. I could tell she didn't want me holding her, but she kept the peace. Since I knew she didn't, I released Candy and took hold of Tamia's hand. "Look, Candy, you're not alone. We got your back. All you have to do is be strong. Getty is a fighter he won't let this minor setback destroy him?" While these were the words that came out of my mouth, I didn't know how much I believed them. I was hoping for the best but preparing for the absolute worst.

"I hope so because I really don't know what to do."

***

That night, Tamia's mother was once again out working her third-shift job. So, I took the time to gather my thoughts in Tamia's basement. I had Two .40 Glocks on the table, and a pound of Miami Loud in front of me. I was just smoking my third blunt when Tamia stuck her head in the doorway that led down the stairs. "Baby, can I come and holla at you for a minute?"

"Nall, boo I'm chilling. I'm just trying to get my mind together. What's good?"

"I got somebody I want you to meet. I mean I know it's short notice, and all that, but I think you should really holla at him." She came halfway down the steps to watch my reaction. "Please Daddy?"

I exhaled, agitated. "Who the fuck is he, Tamia? You know I don't like meeting ma'fuckas the I don't know."

"Well, you know I'm half Puerto Rican, right?"

I nodded. "What that got to do with anything?"

"Well, my cousin Chino is in town from Chicago. Baby, I told him everything that has been happening and I told him how much you really mean to me. He says he's willing to assist you on the strength of me."

I waved her off. "I don't know that nigga, and I don't need him. Tell him I'm good."

Tamia stuck her top lip out. "Please, baby just have a sit down with him. Y'all can get to know each other. Who knows where things might lead? Please!"

"Tamia, I ain't fuckin' wit' that nigga. I don't know him and I ain't tryna get to know him. I appreciate your concern, but for me, it ain't that fuckin' serious. I'ma handle my bidness when I'm supposed too. When I do, trust me, I'ma be alone. Now to tell homie to bounce and lock them doors up there."

She hesitated. "But please, Daddy?"

"Tamia, no, now go!"

She frowned and turned her back on me, before stomping back up the steps. I could hear a bunch of murmuring before the front door slammed. Minutes later, Tamia was coming down the steps with a pissed off look on her face. She took a seat on the couch across from me and crossed her arms. She even had the nerve to poke her bottom lip out.

I tried to ignore her for a few minutes before I peeped her from the corners of my eyes. "Tamia, what's your problem?"

"Nothin'."

"Man, what's the matter with you? I ain't gon' ask you that shit no more." I took a few puffs from my Miami Loud and held the smoke in my lungs. I could feel my eyes turning red.

"It's nothing, JaMichael. Just that I took the time out to explain to my cousin all of the stuff that's been going on. The minute he's down to help you he's snubbed. That's not right." She sighed and refused to make eye contact with me.

"The only reason he ain't trying to fuck wit' me is because he don't know who I am," Chino interrupted, coming down the stairs.

I damn near broke my neck to see exactly who this dude was. I was already pissed he was still in the house after I'd told her to make him bounce. "What the fuck is you still doing here?" I asked, standing up.

Chapter 12

It was eight o'clock at night, two days later when Chino pulled his baby blue, Porsche truck up to the front of Tamia's mother's house, banging Reggaeton. When he saw me coming down her porch steps, he opened the driver's door to his whip and got out. I found the sight crazy because his truck was sitting on twenty-eight-inch gold Sprewell's, so it made it sit up high. Chino was only five-feet-five inches tall. He was golden colored, with long, curly, jet black hair that stopped in the center of his back. He had a lil' size on him that told me he'd either done a bit in prison, or he liked to work out.

When he came around the truck, the first thing I noticed was that I could make out the handles of the pistols sticking out of his plain black T-shirt. He had a gold rope around his neck, with a gold Virgin Mary piece on the end of it. A few moments after he arrived, a van pulled up behind his truck. The van had tinted windows, but if Chino was as large as Tamia was making him out to be then I knew from common sense that inside that van were his Hittas. When he came on to the curb, he extended his hand, and we shook up.

"Say, Pa Pa, I know all of this shit is short notice, but it's like my lil' cousin said, she told me about your situation, and what you mean to her. So, it's only right that I step in and do what I can. Come roll wit' me for a minute." Before he got back into his truck, he made his way up Tamia's steps, circled his arms around her waist and kissed her on the cheek. "You okay?" he asked, brushing her hair out of her face.

She nodded. "Yeah, just make sure you take care of him, Chino. He's a hothead just like you. Please don't get into it with him, that's all I ask."

He hugged her again. "Mamita, you worry way too much. I wouldn't have stepped in if I didn't think I could control the situation, I got this. Go in the house and chill. Make sure you hit his phone if there's any new developments with, Getty." He kissed her cheek and came back to his truck.

The passenger window to the van lowered. A Hitta whose face was half-covered by a baby blue du-rag had rolled down the window and started to speak with Chino in Spanish. They conversed for a few moments before Chino stepped into his Porsche truck. "Get in JaMichael, let's roll for a minute."

I stepped into his whip and smelled the scent of Cool Water car freshener cologne. The Porsche looked brand new on the inside. The leather seats seemed to squeak as I moved around on them before I took place and sought comfort.

"Say, Mane, where we headed?" I asked, as the seat belt automatically came across my chest when he pulled away from the curb.

"You rolling wit' me for a minute, Pa Pa. I just wanna get to know you and help you understand who I am, and how I'm willing to help you." He scooted forward in his seat and leaned his shoulder against the driver's door.

"A'ight, that's cool. I definitely got some questions I need to ask you. You cool wit' me doing that?" I asked, looking in the rearview mirror making sure I wasn't tripping about the van of Animals following close behind Chino's Porsche truck, after a few miles I was most definitely sure.

"I'm cool, you can ask me whatever you like, Pa Pa. I ain't got shit to hide. What's your first question?" He sped onto the expressway and picked up speed.

"What brings you all the way over to Memphis from Chicago?"

He laughed and increased speed. "I was down here taking care of business. There are a few friends of mine that live out this way. Also, there's my little cousin, Tamia. Whenever I travel dis way I always try and stop in to check on her. It just so happens that dis time she was going through something major that she needed my help with. So here I am." He spoke very broken English, it was almost impossible for me to understand what he was saying. "You got any other questions?"

"Hell yeah, I do. What makes you wanna help me? I thought Latinos don't be fuckin' with Blacks like that."

He laughed again and switched lanes. "That's the old generation. Us new Ricans we fuck wit' anybody that's helping us get rich. Outside of the money is always a respect thing, Pa Pa. You respect me, I don't give a fuck what race you are. It ain't about skin color no more. All we see now is green. Now I got some questions."

"Shoot."

"Why is my little cousin so in love with you? Do you plan on doing right by her?" He looked over at me, then went right back to looking at the road.

To be honest I didn't feel like I owed him no explanations. What I had going on with Tamia was my business. We'd already been through so much together. So, for me to have to sit back and explain myself to another nigga about what was taking place with us seemed pointless. Besides, I didn't give a fuck what he thought no way. Instead of being on some straight ass hole shit, I decided to feed

99

into his questioning a lil bit just so I could pick his brain to see where he was going with things.

"Mane, that's my baby. We been sweet on each other ever since we were little kids. That shit ain't gon' never change."

"So, you planning on doing right by her?"

I shrugged my shoulders. "I'm just taking shit day by day. I love, Tamia, I ride for her. That's where we are, right now. Who knows where the future will take us? Why is that so important to you?"

"It's important to me because I'm going to be doing you such favors on the strength of her. I just want to make sure I am getting involved with a man that actually cares for my cousin that's all."

"That's understandable. Well, I do and always will."

"That's all I needed to hear, now we can go from there. I'm pretty sure what I got lined up for you, you're going to enjoy. My people have a saying when a man has you by the balls, you find a way to rip out his heart little by little. Mental pain is ten times more lethal than physical pain. Mark my words on that. Just sit back, we will be arriving at our first destination in a matter of minutes."

There were more things I wanted to ask him, but instead, I fell back. I took the time to collect my thoughts. I didn't know who Chino was or where he was taking me, but I was on board with finding out. I needed to get both Jahliya, and Getty off my mind anyway.

***

I stepped off the last stair of the basement, and directly into a puddle of dirty water. The floor was concrete. There were big cockroaches trying their best to swim through the puddle in order to make it onto the portion of the floor that was semi-dry. Three big rats scurried past my ankles. One of them stopped, and hissed at me, before running in the opposite direction. The basement was dimly lit and smelled of piss, and feces. The stench was so strong I could barely breathe without gagging. I held my weight up by use of the banister. I didn't want to go any further into what I considered a place where people went to die.

Chino squeezed past me and stepped directly into the pile of roaches and water as if it were the most natural thing in the world. He waved for me to follow him. "Come on, JaMichael. I got something that I want you to see," he said, walking toward the back of the basement.

I could hear his shoes suctioning against the concrete with every step that he took. I followed close behind. In tow were his goons. They were about ten deep all of them had blue bandanas covering their faces and guns under their shirts. Their presence made me feel uneasy and safe at the same time. Uneasy because for all I knew all of this could have been a setup. Also, safe because I didn't know where we were but if something kicked off we definitely had more than enough armed men to shoot back at our culprits.

When we finally made it to the back of the basement, I saw two chairs sitting side by side. The people that were sitting inside the chairs had what looked like huge, black pillowcases tossed over their heads. The pillowcases were so big they covered their bodies from the waist on up. They were struggling against their binds with no success in breaking them.

Chino stepped right in front of them and turned around to sneer at me. "This is step one to ripping out your enemy's heart, JaMichael." He stepped up to the first captive that was closest to him and yanked the pillowcase off the person's head and slammed it to the floor. Under the pillowcase was a dude that looked to be about nineteen years old. He was light-skinned, with green eyes. There was sweat sliding down the side of his face. He struggled against his restraints. Chino walked up to him and grabbed him by the chin. "Do you know who this is, JaMichael?"

I shook my head. "Hell n'all, I don't know that nigga. Who is he?"

Chino gripped his chin harder and held it. "This is Mikey's nephew. His name is, Kenya. Out of all of Mikey's nephews, this lil' nigga, right here, is his favorite. So, you already know what that means, Pa Pa."

I didn't, but I knew I was about to find out. One of Chino's men came up to him and handed him a cigar tip cutter. That's when I zoomed into the fact that Kenya's wrists were duct-taped to the chair. One of the bigger goons on Chino's team pulled his fingers apart and gripped one in his grasp. Chino walked up to Kenya and placed his index finger inside of the cigar cutter.

"You wanna find out where Mikey is holding your sister. Then you need to fuck over the people that are closest to him. Somebody knows where she is, and where he's holding her. But you see, right now he's too powerful. Everybody here in Memphis seems to fear him. But the Yaks don't. We're from Chicago, Pa Pa, we don't give a fuck about him or the cowards that follow him." He ripped the tape off Kenya's mouth. "Oh yay, tell me where Mikey is keeping Jahliya, right now."

Kenya mugged him and kept his mouth shut, while two of Chino's men held his wrist and body steady. "I don't know what the fuck you talking about, Shawty."

Clip! Chino squeezed the cigar chopper and I watched the tip of Kenya's finger hop into the air and roll across the floor. Blood spurted into the air and landed across Kenya's Adidas. "Ma'fucka, you gon' give me some answers."

"Ahhhhh! Fuck! Fuck!" Kenya screamed out in agony, hollering like a bitch.

Chino started laughing. "You gon' tell me what I wanna know, Pa Pa. This ain't Memphis, right here. Fuck what you thinking, we from the land of Lincoln," he jacked, already grabbing a new finger while the other one squirted blood. The land of Lincoln was another way of saying Chicago, or that you were from Illinois.

Kenya started to growl. "You muthafuckas. My uncle gon' kill you son of bitches when he catches you. I swear to God on that," Kenya said with his face drenched in sweat.

Chino slowly put Kenya's middle finger inside the device and stopped. "I'ma ask you again, Mama beecho. Oh, yay, tell me where the fuck Jahliya is?"

Kenya held his silence and turned his head away from Chino. "Nigga fuck you, do what you gotta do."

"What the fuck nigga, you think I ain't or something?" He pushed down on the chopper and sliced the tip of Kenya's middle finger directly off. Then he backhanded him, made him spit blood across the wall, and took a step back. "Fuck you gotta say now, nigga? Huh, Papi, say some 'ting."

Kenya was groaning in intense pain. Both of his fingers were skeeting blood. Chino's goon kept control of his fingers. He spread them and held the ring finger out for Chino.

"Let me the fuck go, Mane. This ain't got shit to do wit' me."

"Oh, yay, PaPa, I'm telling you now, where I'm from, it's three strikes and you're out. You done already got two. Now I'ma ask you again. Where is Mikey keeping, Jahliya?"

Chino pulled a .9 millimeter from the small of his back and cocked the hammer, placing the gun to Kenya's forehead. "Last chance."

Kenya trailed his eyes up to the barrel of the gun and swallowed. "Nigga, I said what I said. If you gon' pull that trigger, then handle yo bidness."

Chino laughed. "Me gusto Este negro, Tiene bolas." Translated meant, I like this nigga, he got balls. Chino took a step back and pulled the trigger twice, knocking the back of Kenya's head off.

Chapter 13

I jumped back, after feeling Kenya's blood spatter my face. I took my hand and wiped away the mess that Chino had made. Then I looked down at Kenya. He laid motionless on the ground. A pool of blood formed around him. It spread so fast a portion of it was already at the tip of my Jordan's. Chino turned over his shoulder and directed one of his goons to clean up the mess of Kenya.

"Limpia esta mierda," he said, waving his hand over Kenya's body.

I watched two of his men remove Kenya from the basement floor, before Chino stepped to his right, and pulled the black pillowcase off the next captive's head. This one was also a male. He looked a tad older, maybe twenty-something.

Chino looked back at me and pulled the cigar cutter from his pocket. "Be my guest, JaMichael. You want answers, Papa, you come and get them."

I agreed, stepping over the puddle of blood. I took the cigar cutter from him and ripped off the tape covering dude's mouth.

"Say, Mane, I don't know what the fuck is going on. But don't do me like you just did that nigga," he said before I could even get a word out.

Chino laughed. "Yeah, nigga, silence ain't gon' get you no muthafuckin' where in here. Tell us what we need to know."

I grabbed him by the throat. "Where is, Jahliya? Where the fuck is dude keeping my sister?" I squeezed as hard as I could until I heard him gag. He struggled against his restraints. I let him go and stood back. The basement was starting to smell like copper because of the blood. Whenever blood started to dry up that's what it reminded me of.

He coughed and tried to suck in as much oxygen as he could. "Damn, man, look I already know who you are, Ja-Michael. I know about your sister, Jahliya, but I swear to God I don't know where he's keeping her one percent. I—"

Chino slapped the duct tape back around his mouth. "Cut his shit off, JaMichael. Do it now, we ain't got no time to be playing games."

I forced his middle finger into the cigar cutter with two of Chino's men helping me to keep him steady. As soon as it was inside as far as it could go, I chopped down on it and watched the tip of it fall to the floor. Blood started to shoot from the socket over and over again.

"Ahhhh!" The captive hollered at the top of his lungs. Thick beads of sweat formed on his forehead and rolled down the side of his face.

"I ain't playing wit' you, Potna. That's my sister, tell me where the fuck she's being held." I ripped the tape off and mugged him.

His chest heaved up and down. Tears came out of his eyes and rolled down his cheeks. "Y'all ain't have to cut off my fuckin' finger. Mikey is his own man, I'm just his lil' brother."

I slapped him, hard. "Answer my fuckin' question."

"I don't know nigga, shit!" He lowered his head. "Nigga I don't even think that bitch is still alive. I think he smoked yo' sister, and if he did, that ain't got nothin' to do with me," he said, his voice was raspy and full of emotion.

I felt like I was about to puke. I felt like I had been punched in the gut. I imagined my sister no longer being in my life, my eyes began to burn. I blinked, a lone tear fell down my cheek. "What the fuck you just say?"

Chino covered his own mouth with his right hand and shook his head. He took it away and sighed. "He said, Mikey, killed her."

The captive shook his head. "Nall man, I said I think Mikey killed her. That's what some of the homies were saying a few days ago. I don't know how true it is. I saw your sister one time two days ago. Mikey had her walk through the trap in some red lingerie with her breasts all out. She was handcuffed behind her back. That shit looked crazy as hell. All the fellas were slapping her ass and shit. It was completely unnecessary."

I backhanded him so hard I knocked him and his chair sideways. I slipped and landed on one knee. My heart was pounding in my chest. I could feel my mouth becoming dry from the fear I felt deep within the pits of my soul. "Bitch ass nigga, you mean to tell me you ain't take part in the defilement of my sister?"

The captive was too busy groaning in pain to answer me. A string of blood oozed from his mouth and connected to the concrete. He spit a bloody loogey and kept quiet.

Chino grabbed him by his dreads and pulled him back to an upright position. "Get yo' sick ass up and face these consequences like a man."

As soon as he was upright, I grabbed him by the shirt and balled the material into my fist. "Nigga, I need the address to the last place you saw my sister. I need to know any other places he could be keeping her if it turns out that she is not there. If you don't tell me what I need to know—" I took a hold of his index finger with help from Chino's goons and stuffed it inside of the chopper.

I brought the blade down hard and it took me a few times before half of his index finger was dropping on the floor.

"Alright—alright! Please, man, I'll give you everything I know," he cried.

Chino smiled and nodded. "That sounds like a good idea to me, Papa. A real fuckin' good idea."

***

Two hours later, I was standing at the back door to the trap house in Black Haven. I raised my foot with Chino's men standing behind me. All of them were masked up and ready for war. I held the sides of the door and kicked it as hard as I could, right where I thought the lock would have been. On the first kick, the door splintered. I grabbed a better grasp and kicked it once again as hard as I could, finally it opened with the chain hanging broken on it. Before I could even gather myself, Chinks men rushed around me and into the house on bidness.

Boom! Boom! Boom! Boom!

Then there was fully automatic gunfire. I didn't know if the firing was coming from us, or from what I assumed was Mikey's Duffle Bag Cartel niggas, but there was the heavy scent of gun powder in the air. I took a few seconds, then joined in the fun with my heart beating like crazy. When I first entered the house two of Chino's men were laying on the ground leaking from gunshot wounds. Three more of them were on one knee in the kitchen shooting at the men toward the front of the house. I didn't know where they were, but I started letting off shots.

Bocka! Bocka! Bocka!

Automatic gunfire was returned. More shooting back came from us, then there was a bit of silence, followed by a loud doom! The front door was kicked in, and the next thing I knew the men that had been bussing at us from the living room were now running toward the kitchen. As soon as they came into my line of vision, I closed one eye to aim my gun better. Then I was shooting with bullet shells hopping out of my gun as I released slug after slug. My bullets knocked the first dude back and spun him a hundred and eighty degrees. Chino's men kept on bussing. I slowly backed back out of the house. When I got into the backyard, Mikey was coming out of the trap next door with a handful of Jahliya's hair. She screamed as he forced her to run toward the back alley where I could see a car waiting for them.

Bocka! Bocka! Bocka! He bussed in my direction. I ducked behind the back porch. "You come any closer, I'ma stank this bitch, JaMichael!" he threatened.

"JaMichael!" Jahliya screamed. "Help me, lil' bruh! Kill dis nigga!"

Bocka! Bocka! "Shut up!" Mikey ordered, getting her into the alley.

One of his men ran around the car with a Tech-9 and started shooting with his finger holding down the trigger. *Bock! Bock! Bock! Bock!* He rushed in my direction, I took off running on the side of the house, after sending four shots in his direction. I ran toward the trap I saw them coming out of. I could hear Chino's men taking care of bidness inside of the first house. Gunfire erupted again. By the time I got to the back of the house that Jahliya and Mikey had come out of he was stuffing her into the car and getting in with his gun pressed to the back of her head. The car scurried out of the alley and was gone, taking a major piece of my heart with it.

***

That night I sat across from Chino while he spread a quarter key out on the table and made four thick lines. He took one to the head and gagged. "Shit, this that Ping Ping, right here, Papi. Trust me on that." Ping Ping was another way Puerto Ricans referred to good coke. The pinkish-white substance he was tooting had to be good. He cleared another line and pinched his nostrils together while his men stood around him as armed bodyguards.

"Fuck is we finna do about this nigga, Chino? We were right there, Chino. We wound up running inside the wrong house. Fuck, this nigga don' probably killed my sister by now."

Chino shook his head. "No, he didn't."

"What, how can you possibly know that?"

"Because, if he kills your sister you are no longer an asset to him. All you become is a rival. A rival that he knows will be coming at his head every chance you get, because he would have killed, Jahliya. Nall, it seems to me Mikey got more common sense than that. We just gotta figure out his next move."

I lowered my head. I kept seeing images of Jahliya. She looked like she had lost some weight. Her hair had been all over the place. She looked worried. I started wondering about all the shit he could have possibly done to her already, it made me sick on the stomach.

"Yeah, well, how do we go about doing that?"

He shrugged his shoulders. "All we can do is chill for, right now. Memphis is small, and because of us, it's on fire, right now. We need to lay low for a few days and let me do some digging. When I figure out a few things and make a couple of drop-offs, I'll be in touch with you. Trust me, Papi." He gave me a half of hug and patted my back. "Dat sound like a plan to you?"

I exhaled and sat down on the couch. "I ain't got a fuckin' choice, do I?"

Chino got ready to take another dose of Ping Ping. "Nall, you really don't."

***

Tamia massaged my shoulders as I sat in front of a plate of fried chicken, and baked macaroni and cheese that she'd cooked. It tasted so good, but after every bite, I felt like I was getting ready to vomit. We were sitting inside her dining room, at ten o'clock at night. The plate of food had been sitting in front of me ever since eight. Tamia heated it up three times already.

"Daddy, I know you're stressed, but I need you to eat something. You're steady getting skinnier and I don't like it. I'm worried about your health. Now come on, just let me feed you." She spooned up a nice portion of the macaroni and placed it against my lips.

I exhaled through my nose and slowly opened my mouth, so she could slide the food inside, which she did. I chewed with my eyes and mouth closed. I tried to focus on everything other than the fact that I was feeling like puking. I kept seeing Jahliya as Mikey's prisoner. The sight made me feel like a straight bitch nigga. It was my job to protect and save my sister if things should ever go wrong. Yet, so far, I had not been able to do either. That was insulting to me.

"There you go, baby. I'm so proud of you," Tamia said, before kissing me on the cheek and ripping some of the chicken off the bone, feeding it to me. She even took the time to dunk it in a nice amount of Tabasco sauce. That had always been my favorite.

I chewed as soon as the food was in my mouth. "Thank you, baby. You're always taking care of me. That's why I love you so much."

She smiled and broke off another piece of chicken. "Well, this is my job. You're my man, and you're going to be my husband one day. I gotta do all I can for you, so you'll always know you're not alone. Now eat."

I took the chicken from her fingers and began to eat. In a matter of fifteen minutes, Tamia had fed me the entire meal, and helped to wash my hands after. Then we sat in the living room with her straddling me, sitting on my lap. She kissed my neck and rested her lips against it. "Daddy, I just want you to know that everything is going to be okay. I know my cousin is a little rough around the edges, but he's a major nigga back in Chicago on the Westside. My aunt says he is well respected, and he loves the hell out of me, which is a good thing. He's going to help you get, Jahliya back. Trust me on this, Daddy." She sucked my neck and ran her tongue up and down the thick vein there. "Do you trust me, Daddy?"

Her kisses felt real good. My dick was already rising because of the pressure she was applying to my lap. So, the pressure coupled with the kisses, and licks along my neck were enough to get my engines revved up.

"Yeah, boo, I trust you, but only you. I love you and all that shit. But if yo' cousin fucks shit up, and something happens to my sister. I'm smoking that nigga wit' no remorse, or hesitation. That's on my mom in heaven," I promised.

She sat up straight on me and flared her nostrils. "Damn, Daddy, why you always gotta expect the worst from everybody?"

"Because ma'fuckas are dirty. Why is this nigga doing all of this anyway? He don't know me, and now because of me he done lost two of his men. What the fuck is he gon' do about that?"

Tamia shrugged her shoulders. "I don't know, Daddy, maybe nothing. Them niggas in Chicago be dropping like flies anyway. He used to all of this kind of stuff. It's not a big deal to him," she said rubbing the side of my face.

Her touch felt good, but it wasn't enough to blind me to the facts. "Well, I said what I said? I don't give a fuck how much he helping me if that nigga do the wrong thing, and something happens to my sister. Your family is going to have a serious problem. If that happens what you gon' do? You gon' choose him, or me?"

"I'm choosing you, Daddy, with no hesitation. I'm choosing you until they put me in the dirt." She wrapped her arms around my neck and placed her cheek against mine. "I love you so much, JaMichael. I swear I will do anything for you."

I just kept on hugging her in silence. Tamia was my weakness. No matter how hard I tried to think in terms of being tough or carrying on with a cold heart, she would always say something that would turn me softer than a pillow.

"I love you too, Boo, and for you, I'm 'bout that life. I wish this shit wasn't clogging my brain the way it was. I need a mental cleanse. I love the feel of you in my arms, though."

She looked into my eyes and smiled. "I'ma figure something out for you, Daddy. I'ma help you get your mind right. Mark my words." She kissed my lips softly. "Come on and hold me. I need to feel your body up against mine the whole night, I'm yearning for you."

Chapter 14

It was two-thirty in the morning when I awoke to the feel of a hand going inside of my boxers, pulling my dick out. My eyes popped open and pinned straight onto the ceiling. Then I felt soft lips wrap around the head before half my dick was swallowed. I closed my eyes and groaned deep within my throat. I could feel Tamia's fan blowing on my naked chest. I spread my thighs and allowed the feeling of the sucking to get better and better. The mouth came off my tool, then it was being pumped by a tight fist before it was swallowed again.

My eyes rolled into the back of my head. I took a deep breath and looked down and damn near had a heart attack. Down between my thighs wasn't Tamia like I suspected, but her mother. She had on a red negligée, with spaghetti straps. Her right breast was already half exposed. I could see a hint of the dark brown, big nipple.

I scooted back on the bed, pulling my dick from her mouth. "Tammy, what the fuck is you doing?"

She licked her juicy lips. "What's the matter, baby? You don't want none of, mama?" She tugged on my dick again and sucked it back into her mouth. Her tongue traced circles around the head before she popped it out loudly.

My eyes threatened to roll back into my head again. "Fuck Tammy, where is Tamia?"

She kissed up my pipe and rubbed it against her cheek, then licked the tip of it, and sucked directly on the head. "She went somewhere with, Chino. They said they'd be back in a few hours. I already knew that means the morning sometime. I thought I'd take it upon myself to get some of you, baby boy." She ran her tongue from the base, all the way back up to the tip, and swallowed me whole. My toes curled and I couldn't help making noises I really didn't want to make.

"Fuck Tammy, you gon' make your daughter kill me." I watched her suck up and down my dick in slow motion.

The door creaked open and Tamia stepped into the room. "Nall, Daddy, if it came down to it, I wouldn't kill you for some shit like this. Me and my mother would have to tear this house up trying to kill each other." She stepped to the edge of the bed and opened her silk, pink robe, exposing her cleanly shaved, delicious, brown pussy. She ran her fingers through it. "Damn, Daddy, you just gon' let my mama suck that big thang like that?" I watched her fingers open her pussy lips as she slipped the middle one inside of her hole.

Tammy pulled down the straps of her gown, releasing her breasts. They were so pretty, with huge nipples that stood erect. She pulled on them and ran her hands over her pussy. After lifting them I could see that her box was trimmed. Her lips were just as fat as Tammy's. "Do he really even have a choice?" She swallowed it whole again.

"Hell, n'all I don't."

Tamia kneeled on to the bed and grabbed my dick out of Tammy's mouth and slid it into hers. She sucked it halfway up and down for a full minute, then popped it out. "This my, Daddy's. Don't be acting like you own this."

Tammy rubbed my stomach muscles. She bit into an ab and licked that spot. Her right hand went between her thighs. "Unh, I want him to want me too, Tamia. We can both have him for the night. Let Mama show y'all how to really do this thang." She pulled her nightgown upward and over her head. Underneath she wore a garter, that was connected to her white stockings. Her pussy looked super meaty. She took my hand and made me rub it. She was leaking like a pitcher of ice water in the summertime.

Tamia popped my dick out and straddled my waist. "She thinks I don't know how to take this dick, Daddy, so let me show her. Let me show her that her baby girl is 'bout that life." She reached under herself and took a hold of my pipe.

I held her waist while she slid down it slowly. Her pussy was still tight as a closed fist, but she was so wet that slowly but surely I was able to work myself inside of her. She was hot as a desert at high noon. I almost came if Tammy hadn't caught my attention. She ducked her face behind Tamia's ass and started licking the leftover dick that was sticking out of her. Tamia closed her eyes, then moaned when Tammy's face disappeared between her thighs and started sucking loudly.

"Mmm," she moaned and kept sucking on what I imagined to be her clit, but I wasn't sure because I couldn't see down that far because Tammy's head was in the way.

"Uhhhh! Uhhhh! Mama, ohhh, shit!" Tamia fell back and surrendered herself to Tammy while my dick was still inside of her.

I couldn't believe my luck. This was the type of shit dudes dreamed about happening when their woman's mother was as bad as Tamia's was. I mean Tammy was flawless. She was thick and fine as a muthafucka. She guided my dick back into Tamia and slid to the side so she could have the best seat in the house. "Ride him, Baby girl. You're telling me he's who you love, ride him. Show me you know what you're doing."

Tamia held my shoulders and rode me slow at first. Her pussy was leaking like a faucet. She was still incredibly tight, but at least now, I could get in and out of her with very little resistance. "Daddy! Daddy! Daddy! Mmm-shit-mmm-shit, Daddy!" She tossed her head back and her nipples stood up like caramel spikes.

Tammy wasted little time attacking them. She squeezed her breasts together and sucked on each one of them. I watched her mouth pull and tug until Tamia was screaming and fucking me as fast as she could. This bed was going haywire. The springs sounded like they were being overworked. Her breathing got heavier and heavier. Tammy pulled her mouth away and left them wet and shiny. Then she pinched both of them.

"Ahh, Mama! Shit, shit, shit, I'm cumming!" She began to shake. She fell forward on me and groaned into my neck while her organs rocked her.

The next thing I knew, Tammy had her sprawled out on her back, with her thighs wide open, eating her for all she was worth. I still couldn't believe I was witnessing this. I couldn't help stroking my piece as the scene got better and better to me.

Finally, Tammy arched her back and her pussy bussed open. I could see her lips were slightly parted from the back. I got behind her and rubbed my dick up and down her crease, after taking a hold of her left hip. "Mama, you want me to hit this pussy, don't you?"

She looked over her shoulder at me and ran her tongue across her lips sexy and seductive. "Do it, baby. You the only one that's gon' be able to say you know what both of our pussies feel like." She reached under her stomach and opened them for me.

As soon as that pink winked at me, I could no longer control myself. I took my head and eased into her tunnel. "Tammy, shit ma."

She closed her eyes and slid back into me, engulfing my whole thang. Then she was crashing back into me at full speed. "Fuck me, JaMichael. Fuck me! Fuck me like you do my, baby! Unh-unh-yes-yes-yes," she whimpered, taking all, I could give her.

Tamia made Tammy stuff her face further into her box and wrapped her thighs around her head. "Ohhh, Mama, you fuckin' my man! You're, awww—fucking, my man!" She humped into her face and came hard, rotating her hips in a circular motion.

I was fuckin' Tammy so hard I was damn near out of breath. The constant sounds of the slapping of our skin was loud in the room. She was doing this thing with her muscles on the inside that made me weak. I gripped her ass as hard as I could and pounded into her, drool leaking from the corner of my mouth.

"Shit! Fuck! I'm finna cum…fucckkk!" I hollered between breaths. I came deep in her wounds jerking against her thick ass cheeks.

She waited until I skeeted a few times, before laying me on my back and riding me like a champion. She threw her head back and bounced up and down, while Tamia fingered herself watching the show. Ten minutes later, Tammy screamed and came all over me.

***

I passed out and woke up four hours later with both women in my arms, naked. They were laying on their backs under the covers. I was so petty I pulled the covers back just so I could compare their pussies. I could not believe I'd been inside both of them only hours prior. I squeezed both of their lips together in my fingers and caused them to seep portions of their inner juice. We had showered before we'd called it a night. So, after their juices leaked on my fingers I sucked them off, hungrily, and slid two fingers into each woman.

Tammy was the first to moan. She opened her thighs wider and opened her eyes. "Mmm, every woman wishes they could wake up with a fine ass son like you, JaMichael. If you lived with me growing up, I would have never been able to keep my hands off you." She took a hold of my piece and started stroking him the same way she'd done the night before.

My fingers were a blur going in and out of her now. I was finally able to see up close what it looked like. Her folds opened and closed. Every time I brought my fingers out, they were shinier than the last stroke. She had her thighs opened so wide that one of them was resting on Tamia's hip.

"Uhhhh, shit, baby. I'm cumming—I'm cumming! Damn you, JaMichael!" she screamed.

I kept right on fingering her as fast as I could. She was so wet her pussy was making slouchy noises. It was intense and super erotic. Tamia woke up and sat up. The covers fell off her shoulders, exposing her perfect B cup titties. "Seriously, y'all doing this shit again?"

Tammy bucked one hard time and fell back with her coochie jumping and quivering. "I'm sorry, baby. Uh, but it feels so good. Mama, so sorry though."

Tamia looked down and saw how hard my dick was. Then she looked up to me. "I can't believe you could fuck her with me sleep, JaMichael. I thought you loved me?" She jumped out of the bed naked and ran out of the room, just as somebody started to knock on the door downstairs.

Tammy was petty, she climbed on top of me and slid my dick back inside her. "I can already tell she ain't finna let this happen no more. I might as well enjoy it, right now." She sucked on my lips and started fucking me so fast, I had to hold the side of the bed. Her pussy was doing a number on me. The biting on my neck only made things feel much more intense. In less than three minutes, she was cumming. "My baby, you're my baby. Unh, shit, Ja-Michael. I wish I coulda raised you."

I came as soon as she finished that sentence imagining what life would have been like with her raising me. I saw her coming into my room late at night and riding the shit out of me with those pretty titties, and that was all it took.

After we both came, she tongued me down and kissed the head of my dick. "My daughter loves you, JaMichael. That's a good thing. You gotta do right by her, and good things will come your way. Trust me on that. I'll be there to guide her into becoming a strong woman for you. I know how this hood shit goes. And who knows, maybe even somewhere down the road we can all get together again. I know you'd like that." She kissed my lips again and stopped at the door popping back on her legs. "For now, you need to get yo' ass downstairs, and cheer her up before this turn into a night she'll regret. We don't want that to happen, now do we?" she asked me this looking over her right shoulder. She looked so sexy with her hair all down and shit.

Damn, I think I was just obsessed with sexy, older women or something. "You're right, let me get down there." I could still smell the scent of Tammy's pussy coming off me.

"Yeah, you do just that—" She paused. "—come to think of it. Who the hell coming over here this early in the morning anyway?" She opened the door nakedly, and stepped into the hallway, closing the door behind her.

I stood up, slid on my boxers, and headed out of the room. Tammy was just going into the upstairs bathroom. She winked at me and closed the door. I kept on my way. From the top of the stairs, I could hear muffled voices. One I made out to be Tamia's and the other I couldn't place, but for some reason it got me heated. I rushed down the stairs, into the living room stopping in my tracks at the sight before me. My heart dropped into my stomach, then I just got angry as fuck.

Chapter 15

"Bubbie, what the fuck are you doing here this early in the morning? And Tamia, why did you let her in?" I snapped.

I wasn't ready for all the drama they were about to bring by being under the same roof.

"Why did she let me in? Are you fuckin' kidding me, right now, JaMichael? I'm the one paying your sister's ransom fees and you're going to ask this bitch why the fuck is she letting me in her house? Nigga, how dare you? You should slap yourself."

"Bitch, I know you didn't just call me a bitch, then try to throw in my face what you do for my man? Bitch them hormones must got you all the way fucked up?"

"*Your man*? Bitch, how he gon' be your man when your broke ass can't even afford his situation? Your best bet is to sit this one out. You ain't even on my level in no way, shape, form or fashion. You losing like a runner in second place." She held up her hand. "Dismissed." She rolled her eyes and popped her neck at Tamia.

Tamia stepped back in disbelief. "Who do this bitch really think she is, JaMichael? Obviously, you got her head so far in the clouds that she's losing touch with reality."

Bubbie smacked her lips. "My head been all the way in the clouds way before, JaMichael, came into the picture. Me being with him is just an added benefit to my ego."

"Bitch is that right?" Tamia asked, seeming as if she was over the conversation already. "Well, you can take yo' ass outside and wait for, JaMichael, until he comes out there."

"Bitch, I ain't going nowhere. I need to holla at, my baby daddy. And until he comes out this house I'ma be standing right where I am, right now. And you ain't gon do shot about it."

Tamia lowered her eyes and looked over at me. Then her focus was solely on Bubbie. She took her earrings out of her ear and dropped them on the glass table that Tammy had set up as part of her furniture in the living room. When she'd finished removing them, she stepped into Bubbie's face with her fists balled at her sides. "Look, bitch, I don't give a fuck what you are too, JaMichael. You don't mean shit to me. I don't like you. I ain't never liked you, and you finna get the fuck out of my house, right now." She opened the front door and came back into Bubbie's face. "Bye ho', get the fuck out of my house."

Bubbie crossed her arms. "I ain't going nowhere until my baby daddy comes out of here. I don't know what the fuck he's doing here, anyway?" she asked, without really asking the question to anyone in general.

"Fucking, that's what he was doing here. He came to me because you ain't on shit. That's why you didn't know where he was, and I did."

Bubbie swallowed her spit and looked as if she was being emotionally affected. "That ain't the case. He just fuckin' wit' you because it's familiar. You ain't got nothin' to offer him or no other man. Nothing more than sex and that's fucked up." She shook her head and laughed.

Tamia musta lost her cool because she swung and slapped Bubbie so hard she crashed into the front door. Her face bumped into the side of it. "Get the fuck out of my house, Bubbie! I ain't gonna tell you again."

Bubbie stumbled and fell to one knee. She didn't stay there long. She grabbed the side of the door jamb and helped herself to her feet. Once there she balled up her fists and threw up her guards. "You want a piece of me? Alright, then come on bitch. I ain't scared of you!" she hollered.

Tamia shrugged her shoulders and got ready to rush her. That's when I jumped in the middle of them and pushed them apart. "Y'all chill this shit out. Ain't no reason for the two of you to be arguing like this." Both girls mugged me with mounting anger.

"Tamia! Ta-Mi-Yah! I'm finna kill you!" Tammy snapped appearing at the top of the stairs with a pregnancy test in her hand.

"Holy shit!" Tamia cursed.

"*Pregnant*? You're pregnant? You already know you ain't ready to be nobody's mother," Tammy said, coming down the stairs.

Bubbie took the distraction and capitalized off it. She smacked Tamia with all her might, then tackled her into the wall inside of the living room. They began to wrestle and tumble around on the floor. I was so shell shocked by what Tammy had revealed, I couldn't move from my position.

Tamia wound up on top, she slapped Bubbie across the face twice, then began choking her.

Tammy rushed down the stairs, dropped the pregnancy test, and pulled Tamia off her. "Girl, didn't you just hear what I said? You're pregnant now. You gotta start acting and behaving like a woman."

Tamia jumped up and yanked her hand away from her mother. "Get off me. You got some nerve telling me I need to act like a woman when you know what you just got done doing." She was silent for a second. "My business wasn't your business to tell."

"Lil' girl you better watch your fuckin' mouth. You're still under my roof. You, betta give me my respect."

"Then maybe I shouldn't be in your house. Matter fact, I'm out of here. Come on, JaMichael, help me pack my stuff," she ordered, looking into her mother's eyes.

Bubbie made her way to her feet, her lip was bloodied. She wrapped her right arm around her stomach and took a bunch of deep breaths. She looked dizzy and lost. She somehow wound up in my arms. "Ghost, I feel so weak. You gotta get me out of here."

Her words snapped me out of my zone. "What's the matter?" I asked, looking her over.

"I think it's the baby. Something inside of me doesn't feel right. You gotta get me to a hospital," Bubbie cried.

Bubbie wrapped her arm around my lower waist and rested her head on my shoulder. "Get me out of here, please."

Tamia heard this and turned around to see what was going on. When she saw the way me and Bubbie were hugged up, she lost it. She turned on her toes and rushed Bubbie at full speed swinging her fists wildly.

Bubbie caught two hits to the face, before she slumped to the floor on her knees, and covered her head. "Get that bitch off me, JaMichael, I'm pregnant. I can't be fighting her. Please get her away."

"Now you calling for help? Bitch, you shoulda been calling for help when you was acting like you wanted this shit. Now that I'm on yo' ass you wanna cop a plea. Hell n'all, you gon' take this smoke like a woman." She reached, grabbed a hold of Bubbie's ankle, and yanked her away from me, before straddling her and slapping her across the face again, and again.

I grabbed Tamia up, and carried her into the other room, sitting her down on her pretty pedicured toes.

"JaMichael, get the fuck out of my way. I'm about to beat this bitch's ass for old time's sake."

I blocked her path fully. "No, you not. You're being stupid, right now. That girl ain't trying to fight you. So, get off this bully shit."

She jerked her head back. "*Bully shit*? Now all of a sudden when I get on her ass, you say I'm on some bully shit. Well, you know what, JaMichael. You can take yo' bitch, and both of y'all can leave my mother's house." Now tears were coming from her eyes. I don't think it was because she was on some emotional shit. I think it was because she was so mad she didn't know what to do.

I could hear Bubbie groaning in pain, as she made her way across the living room. When she got to the front door, she hung her head and rested with her arms outstretched against the wall. Blood dripped from her lip onto the carpet.

"Pregnant Tamia?" I asked, taking a hold of her arm.

She yanked it away. "Get the fuck off me, JaMichael. I don't know why everybody keeps grabbing on me." She tried to step around me so she could get on Bubbie's ass again.

I blocked her path, snatched her lil' ass up, and placed her against the wall, pinning her. "Look Tamia, I know you feeling some type of way and all of that shit, but you better check yo' muthafuckin' self before I tear yo' ass up. I'm still, JaMichael, and Tammy is still your mother."

"Get off me, JaMichael! I don't give a fuck who you is, or who she is either. She ain't got no bidness putting my bidness out there. And your baby mother ain't got no right showing up here the first thing in the morning with her sense of entitlement. That bitch ain't running shit over here. That's why I'm tryna get on her tough ass." She tried again to get around me.

I blocked her path and placed her against the wall. "When the fuck was you gon' tell me, you was pregnant? How old is that test?"

Tammy began helping Bubbie, who'd fallen to her knees. That set off alarm bells in my head. She led her to the couch and rushed out of the living room. "I'll be right back. I'm going to get you some ice water and oranges."

Tamia frowned. "I just found this out yesterday. That's the second test that came up positive. I still want my mama to take me to my OBGYN, so I can be sure. Either way, I'm not keeping it anyway. I'm too young to be somebody's mother. I got my whole life ahead of me. I refuse to be a statistic or your second baby mother." She rolled her eyes. "It's enough of that going on in our community as it is."

I didn't hear a word she said after she said she wasn't going to keep the baby no matter what. "Fuck you mean? So, you already planning on having an abortion before you even discussed this with me?"

Tamia sighed. "I ain't finna get on this shit with you. JaMichael, go in there and check on the one baby mother you already got. I'll figure this out on my own, I got this." She looked off and exhaled loudly. "Can you let me go now?"

"Nall, I can't, you ain't having no muthafuckin' abortion. I don't give a fuck how young you is. You can have our child, and I'll raise her by myself until you're ready to step up and be a mother."

"*Raise a child*? JaMichael, you ain't ready to raise a kid. You're still a child your damn self. We both are, but out of the both of us, you're the one least fit to have a child under your care. You got that whole deal with Jahliya to worry about, then Getty, and only God knows how much other stuff. I ain't got time to be playing with my life. So, like I said in the beginning, I'm not having this baby. I gotta do what I gotta do, and you should respect that."

"No, the fuck I don't either. In fact, I'm letting you know, right now. I love you to death, Tamia. You're my baby, and it's meant for you to be my wife. But if you kill my seed, I'm fuckin' you up. I ain't wit' that abortion shit, that's just that. You're not gon' kill my kid."

"Nigga as much hoeing as you do out in those streets. How do you know this baby is yours?" she asked, unintentionally spitting on my face.

"What the fuck me doing out here in these streets got to do with whether this baby is mine or not?"

"It's all about loyalty. If you ain't been loyal to me. What makes you think I should be loyal to you?"

I felt like purging my guts. It was crazy how a man could fuck a bunch of different women out in the streets, but when that one he's in love with even hints that she's fucking somebody else how sick it makes us. I felt like somebody had smacked the life out of me. I couldn't see no other nigga fuckin' Tamia. Just the thought of it alone made me want to kill a million niggas, plus one.

"Bitch who else is you fuckin'? Tell me, right now?"

"JaMichael, Daddy, I need you," Bubbie whimpered, hunching over on the couch. "My stomach hurting me so bad." She looked terrible.

"Go check on yo' bitch, JaMichael. I ain't got shit else to say to you as of, right now." She pushed me back and slipped out of my grasp.

***

It was a good thing me and Tammy got Bubbie to the hospital when we did. She was over dehydrated and in need of fluids. The doctor ordered her to have an I.V. and to stay in the hospital overnight, so he could monitor her condition. I couldn't leave her side. Due to the fact that she was having my child, I felt obligated to be there with her all night. In addition to that, I felt obligated as a man to be there for her. After all, she had come to Tamia's house looking for me the first thing that morning. That musta meant I was on her mind real heavy.

Tammy came into the waiting room after getting off the phone with Tamia and shook her head, just as a text came through on my phone from Tamia.

Tamia: *As much as I love you, I ain't gon' never settle for second place. You can have Bubbie because you've lost me.*

I musta read that message over a hundred times before Tammy grabbed my attention by tapping me on the shoulder. I looked up at her and put my phone away. "What's good, Mama?"

She smiled weakly. "Boy don't be calling me that after what we did. You gon' make me feel some type of way." She blushed and ran her fingers through her hair.

"I ain't tryna hear that. You the only mama I got, right now, so deal with it." I lowered my head and kept on replaying Tamia's message in the back of my mind. I was praying I hadn't lost my baby. "What's good, though?"

"That girl done disappeared. I don't know where she went, but she sent me a text saying she ain't gon' be home when I get back. I'm worried about her." She slid next to me and laid her head on my shoulder.

"Yeah, I am too, she just gotta vent. Tamia will be back home soon, I know my baby." I mighta said these words but I didn't believe them for a second.

After losing Jahliya and seeing what took place with Getty. I felt like I was losing people left and right. If anything happened to Tamia, I honestly didn't feel like I could go on. My brain was already fucked up.

"Well, baby, I'm glad one of us knows her. Because I sure as hell don't no more. I pray that girl doesn't do anything stupid. I'm not gon' be able to sleep until she returns."

I knew I wouldn't able to either.

Ghost

Chapter 16

I helped Bubbie up the final three steps to her parent's mansion and waited for her to open the door to their palace. She put the key inside the lock and stopped. She looked back at me over her shoulder. "Can I ask you a question?"

The birds were already singing in the trees that decorated her parent's landscape. Even though it was barely five in the morning. I could tell it was going to be a hot day. It felt muggy and humid already. "Go ahead."

She placed a slight smile on her face. "Why are you here with me, right now, as well as all of yesterday?"

"Bubbie, open the door, I don't want to play these childish ass games," I said, slightly bumping her out of the way so I could stand in front of the big white door. I was ready to get inside so I could relax. Her mother was out of town as usual. "Come on now."

She twisted the key and pushed open the door, then held it open, so I could walk past her. "Make yourself at home, JaMichael, but you finna answer my question."

"I thought y'all had a maid? Where Shawty at?" I asked, trying my best to change the subject.

"My mother let her have Sundays off. Well, actually, she comes here to make breakfast on Sundays, then she's able to take off. Since she's of town this weekend, and most weekends for that matter. She has been given Sundays off. Now back to my question. Why are you here, right now?"

"Bubbie, because I'm supposed to be. You're the mother of my child to be. It's my job to make sure you're straight, even when I don't want to. I'm hungry as a bitch." I made my way into the kitchen and opened the refrigerator door. The inside was lacked with all kinds of stuff. I grabbed a gallon of whole milk and a box of Honey Combs from the top of it. Then got a bowl, sat down and fixed me a big bowl of cereal. By the time Bubbie came into the kitchen, I was chewing with my eyes closed.

"So, are you saying you really *don't* want to be here with me, right now?" She stopped in the center of the bathroom and waited for my response.

I finished chewing and shook my head. "I'm not saying that. All I'm saying is that since you got my baby growing inside of you, it's my job to ride with you whether I want to or not. As a man, I gotta do what I'm supposed to do."

Bubbie kept silent, she took a seat at the kitchen counter on one of the stools. She adjusted herself so that she was facing me. "Do you wish you was with Tamia right now, instead of me? I mean now that she's pregnant that kind of puts us in the same category. So, I'm wondering if you missing her while you're here with me. If you are, I can understand that, but I want to know the truth."

I took another spoon full of my cereal and ate it. Then I pushed the bowl from in front of me. "Bubbie, what the fuck you want from me? I'm here with you ain't I?"

"Physically, but where are you emotionally?"

"Damn, man, look, if you trying to get the truth out of me you gon' fuck around and get it. Now I'm trying to stand on my own two feet as a man, and hold you down, that's why I'm here. But I'd be lying if I said, I hadn't thought about Tamia a lot over the past two days. She just told me she's having my seed, then we split ways because I left to tend to you."

"Oh, so you're saying this is my fault or something?" Bubbie asked looking offended.

I shook my head. "Shawty I ain't blaming nobody. I'm just saying I made my decision, and I'm here with you. If there's anything I can do to make you feel good, right now, please tell me so I can do it."

"What is it about that girl that keeps you holding on? She don't look all that. She ain't got a pot to piss in and can't be more than a burden all around the board. You got a lot of needs that she can't begin to meet. Yet, you still give this bitch pieces of you I could never get. I don't understand, what is it?"

"Look Bubbie, I'm here with you, right now. Are you sure you wanna spend your time with me talking about, Tamia? Because if you ask me, that don't make any logical sense."

"I wanna know why I don't measure up, JaMichael! Why do you love her more than you love me? Why are you thinking about her, right now even while you're with me? What does she have on me because I don't get it?"

"Bubbie, baby, you're tripping. You need to stop comparing yourself to Tamia. This ain't no fucking competition."

"Tell-me-why-you-love-her-so-much, JaMichael! *Tell me, now!*" she screamed getting heated.

"You really wanna do this shit? A'ight, let's do it then. How about the first fact, she ain't as immature as you are. You're a spoiled brat. I don't give a fuck that you got money, or your parents spoil you. All that means is that you have entitlement problems. You feel like you can get anything you want. Whereas Tamia, she's like me, she straight out of the mud."

"*Straight out of the mud.* What does that even mean?" she questioned, running her fingers through her curly hair again. She looked distressed and upset.

"Exactly."

"Nall don't exactly me. You need to explain what you mean by that term, so I can fend for myself. Don't hold my parent's success against me because all you're used to is a bunch of ghetto losers."

My eyes got so big the skin on my forehead pulled back. "I know damn well you didn't just say what I think you did?"

"Sure did, I ain't finna bite my tongue for you or nobody else. I say exactly what I'm thinking and feeling. If you can't deal with my thoughts, so be it. You ain't the only one that can speak this uncut shit."

"So, that's how you really feel, huh?"

She nodded. "I think you love that bitch so much because she is a resemblance of what you're used to in the ghetto. That bitch is a bum in every sense of the word, and so is her mother. My mother is the owner of the house that they're living in and she says Tammy is late on the rent every other month. Now, how sad is that?"

I found myself getting very irritated. "Bitch, don't you understand I come from a whole line of struggling people. My parents were hustlers. They had to get it how they lived. They took what the game allowed them to have. That's my bloodline, and I'm proud of that."

Bubbie nodded. "Nigga, that's cool and I ain't knocking you for how you feel about your people, or how you were raised. What I don't understand is why is my upbringing, and lifestyle coming under attack? That's what's pissing me off."

"You know what, I don't give a fuck about your lifestyle, or how you were raised. You asked me why I had such a soft spot for, Tamia? It's because she understands where I come from, and what I been through. We done been deep in the dirt numerous times and came out of it together. When it all falls, I know she's going to be there for me."

"And you think I won't?"

"I don't know."

She jumped up off the stool and started walking back and forth. "You know what, JaMichael, let me ask you a better question. Who are you there for when they call on you?" She stepped closer. "Yeah, while I'm standing here trying to figure out how much loyalty I'm supposed to have in order to be with you. Why don't you tell me what you're willing to do in order to be with either myself or Tamia? After all, we're having your children. So, speak the floor is yours."

"To be honest, I don't even feel like going through this shit today, Bubbie. But if I was to answer your question, I'd say that I'm willing to give my life for the ones I love." I felt my heart rate speeding up. "Do you honestly think I'm finna let Mikey get away with what he's doing to my sister and what he did to my nigga?"

She frowned. "Wait a minute, what are you even talking about?"

"Everything Bubbie, I ain't just talking about this weak ass love triangle that I'm stuck in between you and Tamia. I'm talking about some real shit. Like the life of my sister, and Getty. My nigga still fighting for his life, right now, as we speak. Because of Mikey, he might not ever be able to walk again. What type of shit is that?"

Bubbie's kept quiet, she flared her nostrils and looked irritated. While I was really steaming over the subject of Getty and Jahliya. I had previously started with this subject just to divert her from going on and on about Tamia, and both of them being pregnant. I felt like I ain't have time for all that baby mama drama shit.

"Look at you now. You ain't got shit to say, do you?" I antagonized her.

"Yep, I sure do. While you have my sincerest condolences for what's taking place with your people. That don't got shit to do with what I'm asking you. Nigga, I'm about to have your baby, so is Tamia. Neither one of us gets along. I'm not gon' want my child to have anything to do with her and her baby. She ain't gon' let hers have nothing to do with me. You're about to have a serious problem on your hands. You need to make a decision, right here, right now." She walked out of the kitchen and into the room.

"I need to make a decision about what, Bubbie?"

"You need to decide which of us you are about to stop from having your baby. I'm just gon' keep shit all the way real. I was pregnant first, so I should get to keep mine. She should try again at another time. I mean, her situation ain't nothing but guaranteed dysfunction anyway."

It took me a few seconds to really register what she was getting at. Then once my brain understood what she really meant, I got hot. "Bitch, I know damn well you ain't just ask me to have Tamia kill my baby?"

Bubbie backed up. "I ain't say shit about killing nothing. She could give it up for adoption. Or she could get that situation taken care of before there is even a heartbeat. People do it all the time. I'm just saying I think you would have a better chance at raising a family with me instead of her."

"Bubbie, on my mama, I'm seconds away from choking yo' lil' ass out. You talking real stupid, right now. I ain't tryna hear none of that shit. Ain't nobody about to get rid of my seeds. I got this, n'all fuck that, we gon' all figure this shit out together. For now, I'm just tryna chill. Can you be my woman for the day? Can you lay in bed with me and just chill? Let a nigga rub yo' stomach or something. Can we do that?"

She looked me over from the corner of her eyes. "I know you running game on me, right now, JaMichael. I know that bitch is still on your mind. But you know what, I'ma submit, and give you what you're asking for." She reached out and took a hold of my hand. "But before we do, I gotta show you something important."

Ghost

Chapter 17

As soon as I stepped foot inside the nursery, I felt a lil'
dizzy. It felt like everything was closing in on me. The reality that I had two females pregnant at the same time, and
I wasn't even eighteen years old yet suffocated me like an
Anaconda. I felt like I couldn't breathe, I needed to sit
down and take a few aspirins or something. Bubbie held up
a baby blue blanket in her hand.

"Feel how soft this blanket is. If it's a boy he's going
to be so comfortable." Then she held up a pink blanket that
was the same material as the first. "If it's a girl, and I hope
it isn't, she's going to be just as comfortable." She handed
me both blankets, then stood back and watched as I felt
them. They felt like soft clouds, or at least what I would
imagine soft clouds felt like. She walked over to a brand-
new bassinet that was designed by Burberry. "I think when
you and I finally sit down and comes to an understanding
about what we're going to do for the future. We're going
to have a beautiful family. I mean I know we're young and
all, but were smart, and we definitely won't be hurting for
money. I just want us to be happy." She rubbed the inside
of the bassinet and smiled, lost deep in thought.

I imagined a newborn baby being inside of it and began
to freak out. How the fuck was I about to be a father to two
children? My sister was still missing in action. My right-
hand man was laid up in a hospital bed fighting for his life,
and for his mobility to say the very least. I had two enemies
in Grizzly and Mikey that I had to annihilate. On top of
that, I felt like I had so many demons deep within myself.
I missed the mother I'd never known, and I was thirsty to
visit my father Taurus who was in prison. I also wanted a
better future than the streets. My mind was all screwed up.

"Baby, why are you so quiet?" Bubbie asked, sliding her hands over my shoulders.

That snapped me out of my zone. I placed both blankets on top of the changing table and took a deep breath. I grabbed ahold of her hand. "Bubbie, let's get out of this room for a minute. It's starting to freak me out."

She frowned and yanked her hand away. "What is that supposed to mean?"

"What?"

"Why do you look like you're about to lose it?" she asked, almost disgusted.

"I don't know, it just feels like all of this became serious real fast. It was one thing to talk about it, but actually seeing what's going to come into fruition is eye-opening."

"How do you even sound, though?"

"What?" Now I was getting irritated because of how she was looking.

"Ghost, you're about to have two children in a matter of months. That means you're going to be a father of at least a pair of kids, and that's serious. This shit been real. You don't have that much time to man up and grow the fuck up. Ain't none of this shit a game." She rolled her eyes.

"Bitch, ain't nobody said this shit was no game. You asking me why I was looking like I was looking, and I told you why. Now let's get the fuck out of this room because it's freaking me out. Damn, give me some time to adjust to this shit." I reached out for her hand.

She slapped it away and crossed her arms in front of her. "Fuck you, JaMichael."

"Bitch what?" I turned around and faced her. I was seconds away from snatching her up and shaking her lil' ass.

"You heard me, I said fuck you. Yousa bitch! Now what?"

I closed the gap between us quick, grabbed her by her top, and balled it into my fist. "Say that shit again, and I'll slap the taste out of yo mouth. Say it, bitch."

She hesitated, frowned, and tried to grab her shirt out of my hands. "Bitch ass nigga let me the fuck go, now!"

I slapped her and felt like shit as soon as I did it. But before I could feel sorry for my actions, Bubbie cocked her foot back and brought it forth kicking me directly in the balls. I threw up immediately and fell on my side.

I curled into a ball. "Bitch, I'ma kill you," I groaned. "I swear to, God." I could barely breathe.

She kneeled beside me and smacked my face as hard as she could, before jumping up. "Don't you ever put your hands on me again. I don't know what the fuck you thought this was, but you need to check yo muthafuckin' self, quick. I'm a female, and I'm having your kid, JaMichael! You gon' respect me." She stood over me in rage. Her little fists were balled, her eyes were lowered, and red.

I was still feeling sick, she'd kicked me in both balls and sent them up into my stomach. I was waiting for at least one of them to drop but they were taking their sweet time. "Bubbie," I groaned. "Bubbie, you—" I closed my eyes.

One ball dropped, then the other one. I let out a sigh of relief. I kept cupping my jewels protectively. I didn't know what else to do.

Bubbie continued to stand over me. "JaMichael, I don't give a fuck what you talking about no more. You ain't finna let this bitch have that baby. I'm the only baby mama you finna have. If that bitch thinks she's about to have your kid, she got another thing coming. I'm letting you know that, right now. Get yo' ass up, and let's talk about this."

I was already on one knee. When I was able to finally stand up, I let out a groan because I was in pain. I took a step and felt a strange pulling in my lower region. I stopped and closed my eyes. "Shawty if you broke something in me, I'm bodying yo' ass."

"You ain't gon' do shit because if you do anything to me you're potentially hurting your child as well, so let's just stop the shenanigans." She stepped forward and rubbed my face. "Baby, I'm serious about her not being able to have our child."

I took a step back and looked her over. I was trying to see if I could see any signs of her having lost her mind. "What the fuck you mean our baby?"

"Ah nigga, you didn't know?" she grunted. "Since I got your baby growing inside of me, whatever you do from here on out doesn't just affect you it affects me. This baby is our glue. Because of it we are connected as one, and I'm telling you, right now, I don't feel comfortable with another bitch having our child. So, that shit ain't happening whether you want it too or not." She stepped into my face.

I laughed at that. "Bubbie, let me tell you something because it's obvious you think shit is sweet. Shawty, if you keep playin' wit' me I'ma trunk yo' ass and be done with this whole situation. You got me fucked up if you think you're about to be running shit because you ain't. I already told you what it is when it comes to my seeds, and that's just that."

She smiled. "Okay, well, we'll just have to see about that. You've made your position well known, and so have I." She sucked her teeth and looked me up and down. "I love yo' ass, JaMichael, but you have no idea who I really am. Or who you've just gotten involved with, but you'll find out soon. Trust me on that." She laughed and walked out of the nursery. "Muthafucka you belong to me now. Get that shit through your head, Daddy. I'm Bubbie!"

***

Before I left Bubbie's crib she gave me a duffle bag containing a hundred thousand dollars in cash. I was sitting on my bed counting it bill for bill, feeling dizzy, and swearing I'd lost count more than once when Danyelle knocked on the door and opened it without asking me. When she saw all the money on the bed her eyes got big as stoplights, then she covered her mouth.

"Holy fuck, I don't know what you got going on, but I want in. I don't give a hell what I have to do," she said, seriously.

She had on a pair of red booty shorts that were in her gap. They were so tight they didn't leave anything to the imagination. I could make out her sex lips as clear as day. The majority of her yellow thighs were exposed.

"Shawty get yo' lil' ass out of here. And what the fuck I tell you about knocking?"

"I did knock."

"But I ain't tell yo' ass to come in."

"And?" She closed the door and locked it. Then she walked over to the bed with her cut off shirt showcasing her lil' pretty stomach and hard nipples. Her nipples were always hard it seemed.

"What do you want lil' girl?"

"Shid, some of this money. I ain't never seen this much paper in all my life. Not even in a movie."

"You ain't supposed to be seeing it. Get yo' ass out my room."

"And that's another thing if you got all of this money. Why the fuck is you still staying wit', my mama? I would have my own house and cars? You driving some used ass Eddie Bauer truck. Ain't nobody rocking them weak ass trucks. Nigga, this is Memphis, the stunting capital of the south." She picked up a brick of cash and smelled it.

I snatched it out of her hand. "I stay wit' yo' mama cause I'm on something. I drive that outdated ass Expedition because I'm on something. It's yo' best bet to stay in a child's place. Let a grown ma'fucka handle his bidness, especially if you ain't contributing to the cause."

She sucked her teeth and stood up. "JaMichael, I may be young, but I ain't dumb. I'm already all about my money. All that shit you got sitting on the bed is enticing for me. In fact, it makes me horny just thinking about what I can buy with it." She ran her left hand over her stomach and in between her sex lips. "I wanna suck yo' dick, right now. Are you gon' let me?"

My shit jumped even imagining her swollen pink lips wrapped around them. That forbidden shit started coursing through my veins. I didn't even get a chance to answer her before she was rubbing my boxer front, fishing my dick out. She sniffed the head and stroked me while she looked into my eyes.

"What I gotta do to be down wit' you, Cuz? I wanna get my hands on a bag, too." She sucked me into her mouth and ran her tongue up and down it ten times, before pulling me out and stroking me up and down.

I laid back on the money that was spread out all over the bed, while she sucked me faster and faster. She was making all kinds of spit noises that was driving me crazy. I started reaching and pulling her shirt down, exposing her B cup titties. Her nipples looked like pink erasers. They were erect as if giving me head was driving her out of her mind. It felt so good.

"Fuck is you doing, lil' Cuz?"

She popped me out and kept stroking. Because she had added so much spit she was able to run her hand up and down him with no problem. "I'm doing what I'm supposed to be doing. I'm chasing that bag. Now tell me what I gotta do to be all the way down with you?" She shimmied her panties down and opened her golden lips. Her pink flashed, she ran her middle finger around her clit in circles, then straddled me, sliding her body all the way up until her pussy was over my lips.

I started going crazy eating that thang for all I was worth. I held onto them thick ass cheeks and forced her to grind her box into me more and more. When she screamed and came on my face, I swallowed as much as I could, before making her slide down and straddle my waist? She took a hold of my piece and leaned forward with her forehead against my cheek. I could feel the tip of my piece flirting with her coochie opening.

"You gon' put me down wit' you, JaMichael, huh?" She allowed my head to slip into her, then she pulled back again.

I groaned I wanted that shot so bad. It felt hot as a barbecue grill on the fourth of July. "Doing what?"

She slid my dick halfway into her and scalded me with her tight, wet insides, I started shivering. She pulled her pussy off me and bit into my neck. "I don't care what I gotta do, long as you get me right. I'll let you run shit. How does that sound?" She worked my dick back into her wiggling from side to side.

My eyes rolled to the back of my head as she slid all the way down and stayed there. She licked along the side of my neck and moaned.

"That shit sounds good. I'll figure out a position for you. Now ride this dick." I slapped that ass and held her waist.

She smiled, with her eyes mostly closed. She looked so fuckin' bad, as she rode me faster and faster. She dug her nails into my shoulder blades and opened her mouth wide.

"Uh-uh-uh-yes! Yes—yes, JaMichael! It feels so good, oh-damn, this dick—damn!" She held my neck in her little hands and rode me as fast as she could. The headboard started knocking into the wall loudly. I could hear our secretions and sexes slapping into one another. It felt like her pussy kept getting were and wetter. It started oozing out of her and lubricating so much she was able to grind like a porno star.

"Uhhhh, JaMichael—uhhhh, shit!" She jerked forward and started squirting all over me. I could actually feel her jets tapped against my pole.

I started to slam her on me. Money was falling all off the bed and we kept right on going. I pulled her down and bit into her neck. "Fuck me, baby, uhhhh, shit? Fuck me fa dis spot."

She growled and really started doing her thing. "Ooo-ooo- shit, JaMichael! I can't-I can't-uh, fuck!"

I flipped her on her back and started hitting that cat like a savage. I mean I started taking all my frustrations out on her box. I stroked her so deep she dug her nails into my back, and drug them down it. Seconds later, I could feel the blood dripping down it and didn't pay it no mind until I was pulling out, and cumming all over her stomach. After we finished, we sat down and counted the hundred thousand dollars in cash out together and came to a rock-solid understanding.

Ghost

150

Chapter 18

Two days later, Tamia pulled up on me rolling an all red, with pink trimming, Jaguar truck, that had pink and black rims on it. She lowered her tinted windows and hollered out of the driver's window at me because her truck was facing the opposite way of my Expedition. "Ghost! Ghost, we need to talk." I could hear her popping the locks to her whip.

Danyelle was seated in the passenger seat of my Expedition. She gave me a look that said she knew damn well, I wasn't about to leave her behind just so I could go and jump in the Jaguar with Tamia.

"What you finna do, Cuz? I'm hungry as hell, tell Shawty ass you'll be back in a minute," she said, frowning.

I held up one finger. The sun was shining so bright I had to squint my eyes. I turned around, stepped over to Tamia's truck and leaned on the windowsill until it burnt me, then made me back my ass up a lil' bit.

"What's good, Shawty? I see you rolling clean."

She nodded. "Yeah, Chino got me this for my birthday."

I noticed she was dressed all fresh in a tight-fitting Givenchy dress. Her hair was done, all curly. Her makeup was also done. She looked like a billion dollars. It made me feel some type of way. I briefly forgot Danyelle was even in the car. Then all of a sudden it struck me that today was her birthday.

I felt like shit. "Fuck baby, I'm sorry, today is your birthday."

She waved me off. "Don't even trip, my cousin got me right. I need to holla at you, though. Can we roll for a minute?" The sunlight reflected off her MAC lip gloss. Those kissers looked extra juicy.

"Yeah, we can roll, but I told my lil' cousin, Danyelle, I was gon' take her out to get some barbecue. After I handle that bidness, then we good to go."

She nodded her head. "A'ight, well, I'ma follow y'all. You gon' head and get Shawty something to eat, then we can roll-off. Just don't be all day doing that shit." She rolled up her windows before I could snap on her lil' ass.

When I slid back into the truck Danyelle looked irritated. "What the fuck she want besides to give you a headache?"

I shook my head. "Shit, come on, Shawty gon trail us. I'ma buy you some lunch, then go with her to see what she talking about. Cool?"

"I thought you was gon' kick it wit' me today? How the fuck you gon' put that dick on me like you did last night, knowing we ain't supposed to be doing nothing like that? Then don't expect me to be all up your ass on some clingy shit for at least two days? I don't even want you leaving with her ass. I wanna spend the rest of this day with you." She sat back in the seat and flared her nostrils.

"Danyelle, I know I said we was gon' kick it today and we will. I just gotta see why she wanna holla at me so bad. Then the rest of the day can be reserved for you and me. For now, let's go get you something to eat."

"Fuck that food, Potna. I ain't even hungry no more. I'm just about to go into the house and take a nice long bath." She pulled the handle of the truck and opened her door. She was about to get out when she stopped and closed the door back. She snickered. "It's about to be some drama. That bitch, Bubbie's Range Rover pulling up."

I looked in the rearview mirror, sure enough, there was Bubbie rolling up in her lemon and black Range Rover. She pulled right behind Tamia's Porsche truck and jumped out. She was rocking a matching skirt dress that coincided with her whip, over open-toed red bottoms. She walked straight up to my driver's side window and tapped on the glass. I could smell her perfume before I even rolled it down. I took a second to gather myself best I could.

"I sho wanna see how you about to handle this," Danyelle said, seeking some sort of enjoyment from my downfall.

I rolled the window all the way down. "What's up, Bubbie?"

"Nigga, ain't no what's up. We finna go to the doctor so we can check on the state of our baby. Or did you forget about the appointment already?" she asked bitterly.

I had forgotten about the appointment. I don't know how I did, but I had, and I felt horrible. "Yeah, I forgot. What time is it supposed to be at again?"

She rolled her eyes and shook her head. "This don't make no damn sense. How the fuck do you forget about something like this? I swear you just trifling."

"Don't be calling my cousin trifling just because he forgot an appointment. People forget appointments all the time. He's human, fuck," Danyelle chastised. I could see her face getting redder and redder.

"Uh, excuse me bitch, but didn't nobody say nothing to yo' red ass. So, how about you stay out of me and my baby daddy's bidness?"

"Who the fuck you think you talking, too?" Danyelle asked, reaching her head across my lap so she could get as close to Bubbie as possible.

"You! Fuck you think I'ma bite my tongue or some-thing? I'll whoop yo' lil' pretty ass and wouldn't give two fucks about it. Like I said, stay out of me and my baby daddy's bidness."

Danyelle opened the door to my truck and got out at the same time Tamia started blowing her born. I didn't know what to do, or who to answer to first.

Danyelle came all the way around the truck and got in Bubbie's face. "Bitch say something else, I swear to God I'm finna hit you in your shit, right here, right now. I'm tired of you thinking you're so tough and everybody's sup-posed to be scared of yo' ass. You got me fucked up."

Bubbie took a step back, lunged forward, and pushed Danyelle so hard she stumbled back and tripped over the curb. She fell on her side and bloodied her elbow. "Bitch, you betta watch who the fuck you talking, too. I'm tired of y'all testing me. Ain't no ho in my blood, only ho in me is for that nothing ass nigga sitting I'm that driver's seat."

Tamia rushed her and bumped her back. "Bitch don't be trying to fight her. Pick on somebody your own size." She cracked her knuckles and threw up her guard.

Bubbie backed up. "Y'all know what, I ain't come over here to be fighting with you less than bitches. I came over here to see my man. Come on, JaMichael, let's get the fuck out of here. I got some news about, Jahliya." She stepped around Tamia and stood in front of me.

I'd stepped out of the truck so I could at first help Danyelle up, then stop Tamia and Bubbie from fighting.

"Bubbie, what the fuck is wrong with you?" I asked, helping Danyelle to her feet.

Danyelle yanked away from me and took her earrings out of her ear. "Nall, don't ask her that question until I fin-ish giving her the ass whipping of a lifetime. This bitch got me all the way fucked up." She bumped me out of the way as hard as she could and attempted to slap the shit out of Bubbie.

Bubbie was too quick, she ducked, and came back up with a right hook, and slapped Danyelle's face so hard she fell back into my arms. Then Bubbie was kicking off her red bottoms and bouncing up and down on her toes.

"Fuck it, let's get it? I'm finna fight both of you bitches if I have, too."

Tamia kicked off her heels and stepped into the middle of the street. She held her arms out like a cross. "You just don't know how long I been waiting to whoop your ass. Bring yo' punk ass in the middle of this street and we about to get it on like Marvin Gaye."

Bubbie dropped her shoes inside her Range Rover and met Tamia in the middle of the street. Now there were at least twenty people gathered around like spectators. They closed in hoping for the best fight of their lives I guessed. Danyelle continued to hold her face.

She looked at me sad, and weary. "I can't believe you allowed that bitch to put her hands on me. I'm supposed to be your blood." She poked out her lip. There was a split inside of it with blood coming out of the crack.

"Look Shawty, if you ain't about that life, don't go fucking wit' females that are. I don't fuck wit' nothin' weak. This my circle get wit' it or bounce like a basketball." I left her holding her face.

I didn't feel no sympathy for her because Bubbie had bussed her in her shit. That killa shit excited me, to say the least. By the time, I got to the middle of the street, Tamia had already taken off on Bubbie. She had her against the car by the hair, punching her in the jaw. I rushed over and got ready to pull her off her, but Bubbie somehow wiggled out of Tamia's hold and returned her blows. She hit Tamia three times so fast I don't think Tamia felt them until she was falling back and landing on her ass.

"I told you, bitch, I told you. Y'all ain't gon' keep coming for me unless I send for you. Now get yo' ass up. Get up!" Bubbie ordered.

Tamia came to her feet and staggered a bit. She had blood coming out of the corner of her mouth. She wiped it away and laughed. "Okay, bitch, I see what you on." She pulled a box cutter out of her bra and extended the blade. Then she was rushing her at full speed.

I hurried and jumped in the way. "Tamia, what the fuck is you finna do with that?"

"Get out of my way, JaMichael. I'm finna send this bitch on her way. I'm tired of playing games with her anyways." She tried to fight me off with one hand while holding her box cutter in the other.

Bubbie scoffed, "Oh, yeah, bitch? You wanna go and get weapons and shit? A'ight then." She ran to her Range Rover and pulled open the door. The next thing I knew she was out of sight for a brief second.

Danyelle was peeping her every move. I figured she was looking for the right moment to attack. Her eyes grew big as city bus steering wheels. "Ah shit, this crazy bitch got a gun!" She took off running.

Bubbie came from around her truck with a Glock .40 in her hands. It was already cocked, she aimed it at Tamia. "Bitch, now what you wanna do?"

I expected Tamia to take off running. Instead, she stood her ground, and even had the audacity, to walk toward Bubbie with her arms out. The people that had once been gathered took off running in every direction. I shook my head in irritation and jumped in the middle of them once again.

"Bubbie, put that gun away! What the fuck is you doing?"

"What the fuck does it look like? I'm finna clap this bitch. After I clap her, I ain't gon' have to worry about you always dipping off with her bum ass. I want us to have a happy family. As long as this bitch got air in her lungs, we ain't gon' be able to have that." She raised the gun. "Move, JaMichael."

I stepped in front of Tamia and forced her to get behind me. Even though she was fighting me the entire way. "Bubbie, I ain't gon' tell yo' lil' ass again, put that muthafuckin' gun down. This shit ain't even that serious."

"It might not be for you, JaMichael, but it is for me. I'm sick of this bitch. I ain't never liked her and I still don't. The fact that this bitch got your baby inside of her is killing my soul. That shit is making me suicidal, no lie."

"Then bitch put the gun to your own head and pull the trigger. Do the world a favor," Tamia jacked from behind me.

Bubbie tried her best to get a line of fire. She closed one eye and turned the gun sideways seemingly ready to shoot. "Get out of the way, Ghost. Please, Daddy, I don't wanna hit yo ass."

"*Daddy*? You got this bitch calling you, Daddy like I call you?" Tamia snapped. She looked as if she wanted to cry. Just seeing the pain in her eyes made me feel nauseous.

"Baby, that's just something she been calling me. I—" I started.

"Really, you're about to explain to this bitch why I call you what I do? Fuck this." She aimed and squeezed the trigger.

Bocka!

Ghost

I could hear the bullet whizz past us. Instead of Tamia getting spooked she seemed to become tenser. She tried to move me out of the way again.

"Bitch, you wanna kill me then do it. That's the only way you gon' take me out of this picture. This nigga loves me. Bitch you just convenient, it's all about your money, trust me when I tell you that," Tamia spat.

Bubbie frowned and sniffled. "Is that true, Ghost?" She looked up at me with tears running down her eyes. "Are you just using me?" She swallowed her spit.

"Y'all need to stop this dumb shit. Fuck, y'all are about to have my kids. It's time we all act like grown-ass adults," I said, looking back and forth from one female to the next.

"That don't answer my fuckin' question. Tell me are you using me or not? Got damn it!" She wiggled the gun in her hand, before pointing it at me.

Something told me to look down the street to my right. When I did my heart dropped into my stomach. "Ah, shit!"

Chapter 19

Coming down the street were two drop-top, red Mustangs. In the back seats of each car were armed shooters. They had black bandanas over their faces and fully automatics in their hands. Inside the passenger seat of the very first car was Katey, Getty's baby mother. She had a mean mug on her face, and duct tape around her mouth which I found odd. The cars were moving slow, but when they got half-way down the block they picked up speed and started bus-sing at us rapidly.

I grabbed Tamia and rushed across the street with her, then snatched up Bubbie. I don't know where my strength came from but somehow, I had each girl under my arms, running with them as if they were nothing more than foot-balls while the shots continued to ring out. We dove on the side of Bubbie's Range Rover. One of the cars pulled up and the shooters that were in the back began to chop her truck down with shot after shot.

The bullets were chopping it down so bad the truck was shaking from side to side. I could hear gun shells hitting the concrete, and some even rolled under the truck and stopped right by the curb. The scent of gun powder was so heavy in the sky that it had me and both girls coughing up a storm. The shots stopped for a second and I listened closely. When I heard car doors opening up, I grew para-noid.

"Get them muthafuckas. They behind that truck, right there. Hurry the fuck up!" The voice ordered.

I felt a chill go down my spine. Bubbie pushed off me and took off running toward the gangway of the house that was directly in front of us. As soon as she did, I pushed

Tamia down, upped my .45, and started bussing at our culprits.

Bocka! Bocka! Bocka! Bocka!

I loved the feel of the foe nickel jumping in my hand as it spit round after round. Bubbie got all the way up the path to the gangway and fell. She let out a piercing scream that got me worried. I really started letting those rounds off then. Aiming to kill. I locked my eyes on one of the shooters who looked like he was having a hard time holding his AK in his arms. As he spat the bullets trying to aim at Bubbie I hit his ass up two times, popping him in the shoulder, and his left rib. I literally watched the bullets go through his body and exit behind him knocking chunks of his meat on to the sidewalk. He flew back, then jumped up and took off running toward the car that he'd jumped out of.

The second shooter was spraying but backing up as he let off slug after slug? When his gun stopped, signaling that it was empty, he ran and jumped back into the whip that had Katey inside of it. The driver turned to Katey and pressed the barrel of the gun to her temple. Once it was there, he looked directly into my eyes and pulled the trigger. Her brains spattered all over his face, then he opened the door and pushed her out of the car. She landed on the curb lifeless, a big hole in her temple oozing saucy oodles and noodles.

Tamia saw what took place and remained pressed to the back of Bubbie's truck. I could see her lips moving as if she were praying. I couldn't wait for the shooting to start again. So, I initiated the gunfight the second time. I started airing at their windshields, popping big holes into them. The cars skirted off down the street with the squealing of their tires. The scent of burnt rubber and gun smoke wafted into the air.

As soon as they were out of sight, I rushed over to Bubbie to make sure she was good. I helped her to come to her feet. She held her stomach and looked up at me. Her elbows had been scraped and were bleeding.

"Bubbie, why are you holding your stomach, are you okay?"

She shook her head. "I don't know, I don't feel too good." She leaned against me for support.

"A'ight then, let's get you to a hospital. We gotta make sure the baby is okay."

I heard a truck starting up. When I looked over my shoulder, I saw Tamia rolling up her window and storming away from the curb. She sped all the way down the street and slammed on the brakes. She stayed there for a minute. The next thing I knew she was backing her truck all the way up and stopping in front of me and Bubbie. The window was rolled down and from a distance, I could see tears running down her cheeks.

"I guess you made your decision, huh, JaMichael? Out of all the shit we've been through you're going to choose that bitch over me? How could you?" she screamed, then stepped on the gas, sideswiping a parked car and crashing into another one that was coming down the street. She hit it head-on and passed out. Her head landed on the horn and stayed there. There was a constant blaring of the horn that was so loud it echoed for blocks.

"Aw shit!" I walked Bubbie to the steps of the porch that we were on the side of and set her down on the steps gently. Then I took off running over to Tamia's truck. The airbags didn't deploy until I opened the door. When they deployed the one that came out of the steering wheel knocked her head back. She wound up on the side of the driver's door, slumped. I could see blood coming out of a crack in her head, and on top of that I could hear sirens off in the distance. I figured whoever the sirens belonged to, they had to be about ten to fifteen blocks away and gaining ground. I had to get Tamia out of the truck and to safety. I reached across her body to get the seat belt loose. When I pushed in the clicker it seemed to be jammed. I kept on pressing it in a state of panic.

"Daddy, come on, we gotta get out of here. If the police catch you with that gun, with this snow bunny laying out here dead like this they are going to book you. Let's go!" Bubbie screamed.

"I can't leave her, something could be wrong with the baby." I tried again to jimmy the seat belt loose and came up empty-handed. Now I was really starting to freak out.

"Daddy, let's go! If the police are coming they can get her out. Trust me, you don't wanna be here when they show up!" Bubbie screamed again.

I was sweating and trying with all my might to get the seat belt loose. The sirens sounded like they'd gotten a few blocks closer when Chino rolled up in a drop-top Bentley. He stopped beside Tamia's truck and hopped out with four of his cronies. "What the fuck happened to my cousin?" he asked, in a panic.

Bubbie ran over. "Long story short, some dudes tried to kill us. They did manage to kill her, right there. Tamia was upset, she stormed off and crashed. The cops are a few blocks away. JaMichael, gotta get the hell out of here or he's going to jail. He had to do what he had to do. Can y'all take care of, Tamia?"

"Of, course I can, y'all gon' head and get the fuck out of here," he ordered.

I took one last look at Tamia's and kissed her on the cheek. I placed my lips to her ear. "I love you, boo. You're the only one that I love, too." I kissed her again. When I was getting out of the truck, I noticed Bubbie rolling her eyes. I ignored her. "Chino, take care of her. I gotta get the fuck out of here. Her seat belt is stuck. Tell her I love her when she wakes up."

"Let's go, JaMichael. Damn, he said he got her," Bubbie snapped.

Chino pulled a knife from his belt. "I got her Papa, you don't worry about nothin', I got you. Now go."

We rushed to Bubbie's truck that looked like it had been swish cheesed and got in. She started the whip and pulled it away from the curb with a slight smirk on her face.

***

Tamia didn't answer her phone all that night, and I was blowing her ass up. I was even hitting up Chino, but that nigga wasn't getting back to me either. I was super worried about Tamia. I couldn't think straight, I felt like I was losing my mind. Candy hit me up at two in the morning, sniffling on the phone. Bubbie had somehow managed to get it so that we were stripped down and laying in the bed. She had her thigh around my waist and her arm around my neck. She appeared to be sleeping. I could smell her breath as she snored lightly. It smelled of ginger and scope. I scooted as far away from her as I could without actually breaking her entanglement of me.

"Candy, what's the matter? Why are you crying?"

"It's Getty, he finally woke up. He's saying he don't wanna see nobody but you. What type of shit is that?" she cried and dropped her phone.

At least that's what it sounded like. I could hear her wailing in the background. Her sobbing coupled with that of Angel's. I had to wait until she picked the phone back up before I was able to say another word to her. While I waited I stroked Bubbie's hair and made sure that she was snoring, and sound asleep.

Candy picked the phone back up. "Hello, JaMichael, are you there?"

"Yeah, I'm here. I'ma go and fuck wit' the homie the first thang in the morning. I miss, my nigga. I gotta see him and find out what he wants."

"I been at that hospital every damn day since he got there. I held him down like a champion. Why the fuck don't he wanna see me? It's not fair," she whined, then she was crying again. The whole debacle was throwing me off because I didn't think she cared about Getty as much as she was making it seem like she did. "Hello, did you hear what I asked you, JaMichael?"

I looked down at Bubbie. She'd adjusted herself in my arms and forced my right arm to go further around her little body. I waited until she was still to say another word.

"Hello-hello, damn, the call musta dropped," Candy said.

I sensed she was about to hang up the phone. "I'm here, Shawty. My baby mama just sleep and laying on me and shit. I ain't trying to wake her up? She had a long day." I was about to respond to her dilemma about Getty wanting to only see me when she cut in.

"JaMichael, I'm scared, I don't feel like being alone tonight. My anxiety is getting the better of me. Can you please come over here tonight? I'm scared."

I was quiet for a second because I was trying to understand what she was up to. "Say Candy, you ain't got nobody else you can call to protect you?"

"Nope, you know I ain't been living on this side of Memphis long. I don't know nobody I trust other than you. Can you please come over, JaMichael? Please, Ghost, I'll even cook for you if I have too."

Bubbie rolled all the way over and opened her eyes. "Tell that bitch to go and find another one of Getty's niggas to fuck to get back at him. Tell her I said it ain't gon' be you. That I'm yo baby mama, and you with me for the night."

"Tell her I heard everything she said, and she don't know me to be calling me out of my name. You go see Getty as soon as you can. He needs you." The phone disconnected.

I placed my phone on Bubbie's nightstand and looked her ass over.

She mugged me and reached for her own phone. "What, did you really think I was about to let you go and rescue that bitch. It seems that we got bigger fish to fry." She flashed her phone in my face, it was a message from Phoenix.

Phoenix: *Mikey talkin' about makin' Jahliya swim with the Gators. Ain't nothin' I can do.*

I felt dizzy. "What the fuck do he want? I been paying this nigga like clockwork. He supposed to keep up his portion of the deal." I was ready to panic.

Bubbie shrugged her shoulders. "I don't know, baby. What do you want me to do?"

My head was spinning like a top. "Ask that nigga if he knows where Mikey is holding, Jahliya?"

"Baby, how the fuck do I pose that question without looking obvious as fuck?"

"I don't know, but I gotta get my sister back before he do something real foul to her. Do you think there is any amount of money I could hit yo' cousin with to have him go against, Mikey?"

Bubbie thought about it for a minute. "I'm sure everybody has a price. Besides, the last time I was with them niggas they seemed like they were beefing over some bitch, Mikey used to fuck with. It turns out Phoenix got her pregnant. Mikey is pissed about that. I heard Mikey was going to marry her and everything."

I liked the sound of that betrayal. "Okay then, Bubbie, I need you to find out whatever you can? Any bit of information would help, Jahliya, right now. Can you do that for me?"

"If I do this for you, will you promise to make me your wife one day soon?"

All I could think about was Jahliya. I would do anything for her. It was my job to protect her by any and all means. So, even though marriage was the last thing on my brain, saving my sister was the first thing. "Hell yeah, boo, I promise."

"Will you promise to never put another female over me?"

"I do! Now do what you gotta do."

Bubbie smiled and nodded her head. "I'm finna get, Jahliya back for you, JaMichael. I don't know how I'm going to, but I just know I am. You'll see. Watch me play the game as only a true bosset can. She jumped out of the bed, grabbed her phone and walked toward the bathroom, slightly closing the door. "Phoenix, we need to talk, Cuz. I need you to come and get me, right now." She winked at me and closed the bathroom door.

I dropped to my knees with tears running down my cheeks and prayed to God for my sister's safety and well-being. If Bubbie failed, I was going to do whatever I had to do to get her back. Nothing or no one would stop me from rescuing my sister. I spent the next twenty minutes on my knees, begging Jehovah to hear my prayers. For some reason it was like the longer I stayed down there, the colder I felt my heart was becoming.

Ghost

168

Heartless Goon 2

Chapter 20

When I stepped into Getty's room the first thing I noticed was the many monitors he was hooked up to. My homie looked like he was a robot or something. He saw me as I stepped through the doors. There was this thick ass Asian bitch feeding him his lunch, I assumed. She wore a tight, sky blue nursing uniform. Her cheeks looked pregnant from the back. She followed Getty's gaze and took a step back with the spoon still in her hand that she'd been feeding him with and smiled warmly at me.

Getty reached around and cuffed her ass. "You see how thick this bitch is, Joe?"

I laughed as she swatted his hand away and picked up the entire tray of food. She blushed, as she brushed past me with the food contents and trash in her hands. Her perfume was subtle but loud enough for me to catch a whiff of her femininity. I waited until she left out of the room before I addressed Getty. He was still watching the Asian make her way out of the room.

"Say Shawty I wasn't done wit' that shit. Bring yo ass back here!" he hollered.

"Mane, leave Shawty ass alone. That bitch ain't tryna fuck with you, right now, Potna." I walked over to the bed as he was sitting up and gave him half of a hug.

I didn't want to disrupt any of the I.V.s that he had in him, so I was being super careful. I couldn't stand to see my homie in that condition, but I tried not to dwell on that fact.

"Yeah, I see she ain't on dat, right now. But wait until a nigga gets well. She gon' be on my heels then."

I nodded, with a smile on my face and took a seat in the chair beside his bed. At first, I couldn't stand to look him in the eyes, but me looking down and seeing his metal bed-pan was even worst. I had to suck shit up and get past my condolences, or pity for him.

"So, what's good, my nigga? Why you been sending messages for me to come out here?"

He adjusted himself on his elbows, so he could face me better. There was a glare of sunlight coming from his hospital room window that caused him to squint. "First of all, I shouldn't have to send messages for you to come and see me when I'm fucked up like this. A nigga supposed to be at the top of your agenda. I mean, after Jahliya off course."

I swallowed my spit and felt my stomach develop butterflies when he said Jahliya's name. I imagined my sister's face, and what she could possibly be enduring under Mikey's imprisonment. That shit got me ready to murk something. I took a deep breath and tried to keep my mental focus on Getty.

"Well, I was gon' come anyway. I was up here on a regular when you were inside of your coma. You, betta ask these doctors and nurses, they'll tell you."

"They already did, and I appreciate that lil' brother. You already know I would do the same for you. Fool, you already know you're the only real nigga I know." He was quiet for a second. Then he lowered his head to his chest. "I'm paralyzed, JaMichael."

"What?" I didn't know what to say.

"Yep, I'm paralyzed from the waist down. It would have been from the neck down but thanks to these people they made it happen for me as best they could after five surgeries. I mean I still got a bullet lodged in my spine, though. The doctors said if they remove it there is a ninety-five percent chance I will be paralyzed from the neck down.

That bullet is helping me maintain right now as fucked up as that sound."

I couldn't do nothin' but nod my head. I couldn't imagine being paralyzed from the neck down. I knew that would have to suck on so many levels. I preferred a ma'fucka to kill me. Fuck leaving me to suffer for the rest of my life. I didn't even like thinking about being helpless.

"Getty, that's fucked up, damn life is a bitch." I kept envisioning the day he got shot in my mind's eye. "What can I do for you, though, bruh?"

Getty adjusted himself again. He took a deep breath and blew air out of his jaws. "While I'm down like this I need you to take care of Angel and keep Candy straight. I can't imagine my family struggling. I feel less than a man even thinking about that shit, right now?" He lowered his head and an evil mug came across his face.

"I got you, bruh. You already know if I got it, then you got it, too."

"Oh, I know you do, but you ain't gon' have to do everything on your own. I got like fifty gees put up. I knew a rainy day was coming my way real soon, so I planned ahead. But I also need you to get in contact with Katey for me. Shawty got that bread tucked off in a cut for me. She's real one hunnit," he said with confidence.

I laughed at that, he mugged me. "Nigga, you tripping."

"Fuck you mean?"

"Well, first of all, that bitch is dead. Secondly, I think she had something to do with Grizzly's niggas coming for my head. They damn near killed me and both of my baby mothers yesterday. I still ain't got an update on, Tamia. She ain't been answering her phone ever since she crashed her truck on Veronica's block."

Getty forced himself to sit up. "What the fuck are you talking about?"

"That bitch brought some shooters to the hood to stank me while I was with Tamia, Bubbie, and Danyelle. I don't know or she came in honor of Grizzly or what. But I know she's connected to him one way or the other. But anyway, nigga I said what I said. That bitch was foul, now she resting in peace. Life goes on."

He looked dumbfounded. "Fuck! That bitch got all of my money. I ain't got shit now." He held his chin and dropped his head as if he were in deep thought.

"Nigga, I got you. Yo' people good and you are, too. Long as I'm out here trapping you one hunnit. Just stop putting yo' trust in these hoes. These bitches ain't loyal, niggas ain't either, though."

"You ain't never lied about that. But damn, that bitch fucked me over. I can't believe she gone."

I waved him off. "Fuck her. What's the real reason you called me down here?"

"I know where Mikey keeping, Jahliya."

"What the fuck you say?" I asked, in disbelief.

"I said, I know where he keeping, Jahliya. I ain't gon' tell you how I found out cuz that ain't important. But this where he keeping yo' sister." He reached under his pillow and handed me a folded up piece of paper with an address on it written in lipstick. It looked a bit smudged.

I looked it over and eyed him closely. "Nigga, how certain are you that my sister is here?"

"On my moms, JaMichael. I fucked up, bruh. I done got involved in some shit I should have been told you about. Had I come at you a while ago we wouldn't be going through this shit. That nigga Mikey ain't take yo' sister

172

because of the dope she hit him for, its deeper than that. You see he took her because your father Taurus kilt his—"

The door swung inward and in walked the Asian nurse from before. Now she had on black latex gloves, a wicked smile spread across her face, and was accompanied by Grizzly, and two of his goons. They casually stepped into the room and closed the door. His guards stepped in front of the door, blocking it. Grizzly went under his shirt and pulled out a chrome .45. He mugged Getty first, then me.

"Bitch ass niggas, y'all got something that belongs to me. I want my shit tonight, or it's curtains for yo' pregnant bitch, Tamia, and your sweet lil' Angel."

"You got my daughter!" Getty hollered and tried to lash out at him.

Grizzly's goons were on him. They pinned him to the beds and put the barrels of their guns to each of his eyelids.

"Shit about to get really real for both of you niggas. Starting wit' you Getty where is my shit? The Asian locked the door and pulled the blinds in the room. She sat her black bag on top of Getty's paralyzed lap.

"Let's cause some pain," Grizzly advised.

As soon as he said these words, a text came through on my phone. I read over it, before Grizzly knocked it out of my hand, and placed his barrel to my Adam's Apple.

Veronica: *Baby, she's dead! Get home now!*

To Be Continued...
Heartless Goon 3
Coming Soon

Submission Guideline

Submit the first three chapters of your completed manuscript to ldpsubmissions@gmail.com, subject line: Your book's title. The manuscript must be in a .doc file and sent as an attachment. Document should be in Times New Roman, double spaced and in size 12 font. Also, provide your synopsis and full contact information. If sending multiple submissions, they must each be in a separate email.

Have a story but no way to send it electronically? You can still submit to LDP/Ca$h Presents. Send in the first three chapters, written or typed, of your completed manuscript to:

LDP: Submissions Dept
Po Box 870494
Mesquite, Tx 75187

DO NOT send original manuscript. Must be a duplicate.

Provide your synopsis and a cover letter containing your full contact information.

Thanks for considering LDP and Ca$h Presents.

<u>Coming Soon from Lock Down Publications/Ca$h Presents</u>

BOW DOWN TO MY GANGSTA

By **Ca$h**

TORN BETWEEN TWO

By **Coffee**

BLOOD STAINS OF A SHOTTA **III**

By **Jamaica**

STEADY MOBBIN **III**

By **Marcellus Allen**

BLOOD OF A BOSS **VI**

SHADOWS OF THE GAME II

By **Askari**

LOYAL TO THE GAME **IV**

By **T.J. & Jelissa**

A DOPEBOY'S PRAYER **II**

By **Eddie "Wolf" Lee**

IF LOVING YOU IS WRONG... **III**

By **Jelissa**

TRUE SAVAGE **VII**

MIDNIGHT CARTEL

DOPE BOY MAGIC

By **Chris Green**

BLAST FOR ME **III**

DUFFLE BAG CARTEL **IV**

HEARTLESS GOON **III**

By **Ghost**

A HUSTLER'S DECEIT III

KILL ZONE **II**

BAE BELONGS TO ME III

SOUL OF A MONSTER III

By **Aryanna**

THE COST OF LOYALTY **III**

By **Kweli**

THE SAVAGE LIFE II

By **J-Blunt**

KING OF NEW YORK V

COKE KINGS IV

BORN HEARTLESS II

By **T.J. Edwards**

GORILLAZ IN THE BAY IV

De'Kari

THE STREETS ARE CALLING II

Duquie Wilson

KINGPIN KILLAZ IV

STREET KINGS III

PAID IN BLOOD III

CARTEL KILLAZ II

Hood Rich

SINS OF A HUSTLA II

ASAD

TRIGGADALE III

Elijah R. Freeman

KINGZ OF THE GAME IV

Playa Ray
SLAUGHTER GANG IV
RUTHLESS HEART II
By Willie Slaughter
THE HEART OF A SAVAGE II
By Jibril Williams
FUK SHYT II
By Blakk Diamond
THE DOPEMAN'S BODYGAURD II
By Tranay Adams
TRAP GOD II
By Troublesome
YAYO II
A SHOOTER'S AMBITION
By S. Allen
GHOST MOB
Stilloan Robinson
KINGPIN DREAMS
By Paper Boi Rari
CREAM
By Yolanda Moore
SON OF A DOPE FIEND II
By Renta
FOREVER GANGSTA
By Adrian Dulan
LOYALTY AIN'T PROMISED
By Keith Williams

THE PRICE YOU PAY FOR LOVE
By Destiny Skai
THE LIFE OF A HOOD STAR
By Rashia Wilson

Available Now

RESTRAINING ORDER **I & II**
By **CA$H & Coffee**
LOVE KNOWS NO BOUNDARIES **I II & III**
By **Coffee**
RAISED AS A GOON I, II, III & IV
BRED BY THE SLUMS I, II, III
BLAST FOR ME I & II
ROTTEN TO THE CORE I II III
A BRONX TALE I, II, III
DUFFEL BAG CARTEL I II III
HEARTLESS GOON
A SAVAGE DOPEBOY
HEARTLESS GOON I II
By **Ghost**
LAY IT DOWN **I & II**
LAST OF A DYING BREED
BLOOD STAINS OF A SHOTTA I & II
By **Jamaica**
LOYAL TO THE GAME
LOYAL TO THE GAME II

LOYAL TO THE GAME III
LIFE OF SIN I, II III
By **TJ & Jelissa**
BLOODY COMMAS I & II
SKI MASK CARTEL I II & III
KING OF NEW YORK I II,III IV
RISE TO POWER I II III
COKE KINGS I II III
BORN HEARTLESS
By **T.J. Edwards**
IF LOVING HIM IS WRONG…I & II
LOVE ME EVEN WHEN IT HURTS I II III
By **Jelissa**
WHEN THE STREETS CLAP BACK I & II III
By **Jibril Williams**
A DISTINGUISHED THUG STOLE MY HEART I II & III
LOVE SHOULDN'T HURT I II III IV
RENEGADE BOYS I II III IV
By **Meesha**
A GANGSTER'S CODE I &, II III
A GANGSTER'S SYN I II III
THE SAVAGE LIFE
By **J-Blunt**
PUSH IT TO THE LIMIT
By **Bre' Hayes**
BLOOD OF A BOSS **I, II, III, IV, V**
SHADOWS OF THE GAME

Ghost

By **Askari**

THE STREETS BLEED MURDER **I, II & III**

THE HEART OF A GANGSTA I II& III

By **Jerry Jackson**

CUM FOR ME

CUM FOR ME 2

CUM FOR ME 3

CUM FOR ME 4

CUM FOR ME 5

An **LDP Erotica Collaboration**

BRIDE OF A HUSTLA **I II & II**

THE FETTI GIRLS **I, II& III**

CORRUPTED BY A GANGSTA I, II III, IV

BLINDED BY HIS LOVE

By **Destiny Skai**

WHEN A GOOD GIRL GOES BAD

By **Adrienne**

THE COST OF LOYALTY I II

By Kweli

A GANGSTER'S REVENGE **I II III & IV**

THE BOSS MAN'S DAUGHTERS

THE BOSS MAN'S DAUGHTERS II

THE BOSSMAN'S DAUGHTERS III

THE BOSSMAN'S DAUGHTERS IV

THE BOSS MAN'S DAUGHTERS **V**

A SAVAGE LOVE **I & II**

BAE BELONGS TO ME I II

A HUSTLER'S DECEIT I, II, III

WHAT BAD BITCHES DO I, II, III

SOUL OF A MONSTER I II

KILL ZONE

By **Aryanna**

A KINGPIN'S AMBITON

A KINGPIN'S AMBITION **II**

I MURDER FOR THE DOUGH

By **Ambitious**

TRUE SAVAGE

TRUE SAVAGE II

TRUE SAVAGE **III**

TRUE SAVAGE **IV**

TRUE SAVAGE **V**

TRUE SAVAGE **VI**

By **Chris Green**

A DOPEBOY'S PRAYER

By **Eddie "Wolf" Lee**

THE KING CARTEL **I, II & III**

By **Frank Gresham**

THESE NIGGAS AIN'T LOYAL **I, II & III**

By **Nikki Tee**

GANGSTA SHYT **I II &III**

By **CATO**

THE ULTIMATE BETRAYAL

By **Phoenix**

BOSS'N UP **I , II & III**

Ghost

By **Royal Nicole**
I LOVE YOU TO DEATH
By **Destiny J**
I RIDE FOR MY HITTA
I STILL RIDE FOR MY HITTA
By **Misty Holt**
LOVE & CHASIN' PAPER
By **Qay Crockett**
TO DIE IN VAIN
SINS OF A HUSTLA
By **ASAD**
BROOKLYN HUSTLAZ
By **Boogsy Morina**
BROOKLYN ON LOCK I & II
By **Sonovia**
GANGSTA CITY
By **Teddy Duke**
A DRUG KING AND HIS DIAMOND I & II III
A DOPEMAN'S RICHES
HER MAN, MINE'S TOO I, II
CASH MONEY HO'S
By **Nicole Goosby**
TRAPHOUSE KING **I II & III**
KINGPIN KILLAZ I II III
STREET KINGS I II
PAID IN BLOOD **I II**
CARTEL KILLAZ

By **Hood Rich**
LIPSTICK KILLAH **I, II, III**
CRIME OF PASSION I & II
By **Mimi**
STEADY MOBBN' **I, II, III**
By **Marcellus Allen**
WHO SHOT YA **I, II, III**
SON OF A DOPE FIEND
Renta
GORILLAZ IN THE BAY **I II III**
DE'KARI
TRIGGADALE I II
Elijah R. Freeman
GOD BLESS THE TRAPPERS I, II, III
THESE SCANDALOUS STREETS I, II, III
FEAR MY GANGSTA I, II, III
THESE STREETS DON'T LOVE NOBODY I, II
BURY ME A G I, II, III, IV, V
A GANGSTA'S EMPIRE I, II, III, IV
THE DOPEMAN'S BODYGAURD
Tranay Adams
THE STREETS ARE CALLING
Duquie Wilson
MARRIED TO A BOSS… I II III
By Destiny Skai & Chris Green
KINGZ OF THE GAME I II III
Playa Ray

Ghost

SLAUGHTER GANG I II III

RUTHLESS HEART

By Willie Slaughter

THE HEART OF A SAVAGE

By Jibril Williams

FUK SHYT

By Blakk Diamond

DON'T F#CK WITH MY HEART I II

By Linnea

ADDICTED TO THE DRAMA I II III

By Jamila

YAYO

By S. Allen

TRAP GOD

By Troublesome

<u>BOOKS BY LDP'S CEO, CA$H</u>

<u>TRUST IN NO MAN</u>

<u>TRUST IN NO MAN 2</u>

<u>TRUST IN NO MAN 3</u>

<u>BONDED BY BLOOD</u>

<u>SHORTY GOT A THUG</u>

<u>THUGS CRY</u>

<u>THUGS CRY 2</u>

<u>THUGS CRY 3</u>

<u>TRUST NO BITCH</u>

<u>TRUST NO BITCH 2</u>

<u>TRUST NO BITCH 3</u>

<u>TIL MY CASKET DROPS</u>

<u>RESTRAINING ORDER</u>

<u>RESTRAINING ORDER 2</u>

<u>IN LOVE WITH A CONVICT</u>

<u>Coming Soon</u>

BONDED BY BLOOD 2

BOW DOWN TO MY GANGSTA

Ghost